Chilling. Ogburn has given us a bioethical nightmare that is all too plausible.

James Scott Bell, novelist

Author of *Circumstantial Evidence* and *Final Witness*

Martha Ogburn has pulled off a rare feat for a first-time novelist—lean prose that races with the energy of Grisham or Clancy; a plot that twists and turns, shocks and surprises; personal relationships that push the limits of betrayal and forgiveness. As a medical professional, Martha Ogburn knows her field. As a Christian, she understands redemption and grace. Intrepidly, she peers into what may well be the future of reproductive technology. She disturbs our complacency. She prods us to face issues that we may prefer to dodge and that the Captains of Reproductive Commerce would rather keep from public debate. *Progeny* is as current as today's biotechnical headlines, yet its wisdom is eternal. It'll make you cry, keep you awake, make you pray. Don't start reading unless you're prepared to finish it in one sitting!

Una McManus

Author of *Wild Irish Roses, Tender Remembrance,*

and *Love's Tender Gift*

As a professional in the medical field, Ogburn gives us an insider's view of the trauma of abortion, as well as the financial motivations driving in-vitro fertilization, cloning, and fetal-tissue research.

Bill Myers

Author of *Blood in Heaven*

Progeny

a Novel

Progeny

a Novel

Martha Ogburn

BROADMAN
& HOLMAN
PUBLISHERS
Nashville, Tennessee

0-8054-1889-X

Published by Broadman & Holman Publishers, Nashville, Tennessee
Acquisitions and Development Editor: Leonard G. Goss
Page Design and Typesetting: PerfecType, Nashville, Tennessee

Dewey Decimal Classification: 813
Subject Heading: NOVEL/MEDICAL SUSPENSE
Library of Congress Card Catalog Number: 98-40784

Scripture quotations are from
the New King James Version, copyright © 1979, 1980, 1982,
Thomas Nelson, Inc., Publishers.

Library of Congress Cataloging-in-Publication Data

Ogburn, Martha D., 1952–
    Progeny : a medical suspense novel / by Martha D. Ogburn.
    p. cm.
    ISBN 0-8054-1889-X
    I. Title.
    PS3565.G34 P76   1999
    813'.54--ddc21

                                                        98-40784
                                                        CIP

1 2 3 4 5 03 02 01 00 99

"A voice was heard in Ramah,
Lamentation and bitter weeping,
Rachel weeping for her children,
Refusing to be comforted for her children,
Because they are no more."
Jeremiah 31:15

Contents

Prologue

The Washington Sheraton ballroom was packed. The National Institute of Health Awards banquet always drew large crowds, and tonight was no exception. Renowned for recognizing the best minds and the most promising researchers in the U.S., an NIH award was a highly coveted item. Simply receiving an award was an accomplishment in itself.

Print and broadcast media were on hand, clamoring for space up front as they strategically situated themselves for the announcements. And since rumors of an imminent protest had recently surfaced, extra security guards quietly patrolled the perimeter, scrutinizing guests for possible trouble. Predictably, the promise of confrontation excited the media, and they were already circling like vultures, ready to devour whatever prey might appear.

All the top names in academic medicine had gathered in the nation's capitol. Among them was Dr. Robert Chan, a hardened-looking gentleman of fifty-five with silver hair, spectacles, and definite Asian roots. Although Chan was slated to receive this year's prize in maternal-fetal medicine, the scowl on his face betrayed his lack of enthusiasm. He sat stoically beside his business partner—Dr. Forrest Prescott, director of operations for Biotechnologies Research International— impatiently tapping his fork against the table.

Both Chan and Prescott resented the attention the NIH ceremony generated. They had worked hard to keep their research as inconspicuous as possible, and tonight's announcement jeopardized that goal. But it was more than a privacy issue for Chan; he was actually embarrassed by the accolades, knowing his colleagues visiting from mainland China would not be dazzled in the least by the proceedings. China's proletariat never pandered to physicians like this. It was one's duty to perform for the state; the self never came into play. Awards were nonexistent.

As he waited for the formalities to ensue, Chan shifted nervously in his chair and tried to read the nonverbal responses of his guests seated nearby. Because he was a first-generation American whose parents had taken great pains to instill the Chinese way, he understood—without a doubt—how they and others viewed such a ceremony. Personally, he viewed it as a necessary evil, tolerating it for one reason and one reason only: money. The NIH grant accompanying the award exceeded all expectations and made it possible to expand U.S. operations.

The awards presentation began on schedule. One by one, individual researchers accepted their prizes. Chan, preoccupied with concerns about future collaborations with his Chinese connection, almost missed his cue to go forward—forcing Prescott to nudge him just as the announcement was made.

"Receiving the prize in maternal-fetal medicine for his research in tissue transplantation is Dr. Robert Chan." The crowd broke into thunderous applause, and the presenter paused while Dr. Chan made his way to the front of the ballroom. Once the noise level diminished, the presenter shook hands with Chan, then resumed his prepared presentation, "Well-respected in his field, Dr. Chan's pioneering work in reproductive technology has amazed us all. Now, he has surpassed expectations, treading foot in an emerging area that shows imminent promise for the entire human race. . . ."

Before he could finish his monologue, an attractive young journalist with Asian features jumped to her feet and burst forth with a question, "Dr. Chan, would you agree that the medical profession is experiencing an ethical free fall?"

The question caught both the presenter and Dr. Chan off guard—not because the interruption was disruptive but because the question itself was completely unexpected. Dr. Chan regained his composure first.

"Excuse me?"

The young woman, dressed stylishly in an emerald-green suit, seemed pleased with her ability to assume control of the meeting. She took advantage of the attention and without hesitation continued her line of questioning.

"As a physician, why do you willingly violate the Hippocratic oath—no longer treating the human body as sacred but rather as a commodity to be bought, harvested, and sold?"

By now, a hint of recognition flickered in Chan's mind. Was she the same woman who had accosted him earlier outside his lab? It was dark, and he had been in a hurry. Yet her intense green eyes registered familiarity. And although her rhetoric sounded vaguely familiar as well, with this line of questioning, he felt sure she wasn't an approved reporter. He ignored her last question and stared vainly at the press badge attached to her lapel. Unable to make out anything but "Helen," Chan finally eyed her sternly and fired off his own question.

"Which news service do you represent?"

"Why don't you answer my question?" She held firm, dodging his question with another one of her own.

Dr. Chan, somewhat amused by the cat-and-mouse exchange, played along as the presenter motioned for the security guards. "I'll be glad to answer any questions you may have, but this is not the forum. We can set up another time." He glanced over at the guards who were working their way towards the woman.

"Right!" The woman responded sarcastically, her voice rising. "I know how your men keep you insulated from the public and how you have no intention of addressing my concerns. America deserves to hear the truth about what you're doing—without the spin the media puts on it." She tore off her press badge and threw it on the floor in contempt.

"There's no need to get hysterical." Chan remained calm, his patronizing tone evident to all as the guards firmly took hold of the woman and escorted her out of the ballroom.

The woman, intent on inflicting one last jab, momentarily resisted her escorts and, twisting around, yelled back at Chan, "Explain where you get the tissue for your research. Tell that one to the public!"

A Different World

Dr. Matthew Hamilton had a guilty conscience. And although he'd never admit it, prescribing barbiturates was more for his peace of mind than for Rachel's. Never mind that a disrupted REM cycle negatively affected Rachel's career. Never mind that she had to press that much harder to function after a night without REM sleep. That didn't seem to matter. What mattered was that the

7

drugs kept things somewhat "normal" for him, and "normal" meant pursuing his career without undue interruption and distraction.

Like most of his colleagues, Matt's work consumed him. It had been that way since college. The pressure to become a doctor originated from his father, an internationally respected neurosurgeon; and Matt knew exactly what was expected of him. But knowing was the easy part; reaching the predetermined goal was another matter entirely, requiring a tremendous amount of perseverance.

First, there was the push to get into medical school. Then, after memorizing every medical science textbook available and securing a match at a reputable training program, Matt had to survive an additional four years of a slave-labor residency, followed by two years of a neurophysiology fellowship.

Developing a workaholic mentality was inevitable. It had to be that way. Keeping straight A's throughout four years at Johns Hopkins wasn't easy, and Matt had lots of competition for medical school slots. It was the lab position the summer of his junior year that put him over the edge and clinched his acceptance into med school at the University of North Carolina. It was also the lab position that gave him a brief reprieve from the excessive demands of medical education and training.

National Institute of Health brochures, plastered on bulletin boards throughout the biology department at Hopkins, publicized summer internships at various universities across the U.S. Intrigued by the research opportunities and enticed by the grant money, Matt applied for and landed a position working for Dr. Robert Chan at UNC-Chapel Hill. The first time he drove down the oak-lined streets of Chapel Hill, Matt instinctively knew he belonged. A charming college town with the advantages of a major medical center, he immediately understood why Chapel Hill was called "the southern part of heaven." Franklin Street, the main thoroughfare and a popular hangout, held a special fascination for the locals as well as the students. It was there that two worlds collided: the academic and the community. The flower carts stationed outside the shops contributed to the quaint small-town atmosphere, while the head shops, filled with black-light posters, trinkets, and assorted paraphernalia, did their part to keep pace with the hippie culture. There was always something to do along Franklin Street, where an unexplainable electricity was ever present.

That summer in Chapel Hill proved pivotal for Matt's career, as well as for his personal life. He wasn't looking to forge a relationship; it just happened. Rachel entered his world unexpectedly and, some might say, providentially.

P r o g e n y

The day had been a scorcher. Although almost 7 P.M., the torrid summer sun continued to singe the campus. After leaving an air-conditioned building, Matt welcomed a light breeze. It made the humidity almost bearable. He had worked late that day, finishing up the research protocol rather than stopping to eat, and it was no wonder he was starving as he made his way across the quad toward Franklin Street. His blue polo shirt was sticking to his skin, and the hunger pangs were gnawing nonstop. That's when he spied the accident waiting to happen: a black lab puppy retrieving a frisbee stopped suddenly at a blanket where a small child was eating a cookie. In a split second, before anyone knew what was happening, the dog lunged for the cookie, toppling the little girl in the process. The child's screams alerted everyone, but Matt was the first on the scene, effortlessly pulling the dog away and rescuing the terrified child.

"Thank you," a striking, petite, dark-eyed girl said as she lifted the child from Matt's strong arms. Then, shifting her attention away from Matt to her small charge, she gently brushed away the tears and spoke softly in a soothing voice, "There, there, the mean, old doggy's gone." Nodding toward Matt she continued, "Tell this nice man 'thank you.'" The child didn't respond, her cries changing to a monotonous moaning in sync with the repetitive, rocking motion against her caretaker's body. With an apologetic look, the young woman with the penetrating eyes looked up at Matt and offered an explanation. "Don't take it personally; she's autistic."

"Oh, I wasn't . . . I didn't notice . . . I mean, I don't know much about children." Matt felt increasingly self-conscious.

"You did fine. I really appreciate your quick response. I should've been paying closer attention . . . just too wrapped up in my reading." She waved her arms toward the open books spread out on the blanket.

"Glad I could help." Matt backed away and turned to leave. He didn't belong in this picture, yet he felt strangely drawn to this woman who seemed so unlike himself. While he looked the part of an uptight, conservative, med-student-wanna-be, she fit the free-spirit mold. Clad in sandals, a long, flowing, flowered skirt complete with a psychedelic yellow tank top and deep, rich, auburn hair reaching to her waist, she represented a totally different world.

"Wait, I should at least introduce myself," the young woman said extending her hand for Matt to shake. "I'm Rachel Duncan and this is Emily."

"I'm Matt . . . Matt Hamilton," he stammered, taking her tiny, delicate, outstretched hand in his. Caught off guard by her assertiveness, he fumbled for words. "Your . . . daughter's real cute."

"Emily? She's not my daughter. I'm baby-sitting for my psychology professor."

"Excuse me . . . I thought. . . ."

"Honest mistake. No problem." Rachel tilted her head and flashed a smile. "So, what do you do when you're not rescuing damsels in distress?"

"I work in Dr. Chan's lab, an internship." Matt maintained a matter-of-fact tone, purposely resisting her charm.

"The infamous Dr. Chan? The Dr. Chan I had for biology, except the teaching assistant taught most of his lectures?"

"Probably so. He's so absorbed with his research, he has little time for teaching."

"Hmm. . . ." Rachel mused. "So you're doing an internship with Chan. What exactly do you do?"

"You wouldn't find it interesting. Just studying the embryology of fruit flies."

"Meaning, you watch fruit flies reproduce," Rachel stated knowingly, obviously impressed with her own understanding of the subject matter.

"It's a little more involved than that. Chan is looking into how cells divide at different stages and why mutations occur."

"What does he hope to accomplish?"

"If you take the principles and apply it to humans, I guess he'll learn more about fetal development."

"Now that could be interesting. Let me know when he gets to that point."

"He does some work in that area already. I don't know exactly what, though. I'm stuck in the lab, not the clinical research unit at the hospital."

"You mean he has patients? I thought he was just a biologist."

"He is, but he's also an obstetrical specialist. Has a Ph.D./M.D."

"Smart man."

"Without a doubt."

Mesmerized by Rachel's natural beauty, Matt found himself doing something out of the ordinary, something impulsive. "Look, I'm going to the Carolina Café to get something to eat. Would you and Emily like to join me?"

Rachel looked down at her watch, "Didn't realize it was so late. No wonder I'm so hungry." Almost as an after-thought, she added, "We'd love to join you." Then, as if it were the most natural thing to do, she handed Emily to Matt, bent over and gathered her books.

Matt devoured his burger and Coke while Rachel downed her favorite sandwich on the menu: avocado melt with sprouts. Little Emily sat content in the high chair, gnaw-ing a bread stick, oblivious to the chatter around her. Carly Simon crooned in the background: "You're so vain. I bet you think this song is about you, don't you, don't you. . . ." Rachel caught herself humming along with the lyrics, wondering what drove the quiet, unassuming guy who had just entered her world. He possessed a gentleness that was difficult to grasp, a subtle strength that made her feel safe. He was differ-ent, so unlike other guys intent on making an impression.

"So, am I correct to assume you're majoring in bio-logy?" Rachel began her line of questioning.

"No. Pre-med." Matt's answer was cut-and-dried.

Trying another angle, Rachel continued her interrogation. "Does the fact that you don't have a southern accent mean you're a Yankee?"

"Not officially."

"Not officially? What'd you mean by that?"

"I was raised below the Mason-Dixon line."

"Oh. . . ." Rachel nodded as if she understood. Then when Matt failed to volunteer further information, she realized she'd have to dig deeper to get a more elaborate response from this guy—this guy whose clear blue eyes matched the color of his shirt.

The conversation stalled momentarily as Rachel handed Emily a piece of apple to gnaw on, and Matt gulped down more Coke. All the while, he was deliberating over what he should say next. Even though he knew the ball was in his court, small talk just didn't come easily. Fortunately, he spied the title of a book wedged into Rachel's knapsack—*Psychology of Early Childhood Disorders*—and was ready to enter the game once more. "So you're a psych major," he declared, pleased with his perception.

Catching his glance at her books, Rachel quickly corrected his assumption. "No, journalism. I'm reading up on autism, wanted to understand Emily better. Actually, it's pretty interesting, and I'll probably write an article on it."

"Journalism, eh?" He gave her a once-over.

"Is there a problem with that?" Rachel frowned, not following his thinking.

"I just don't know any journalism majors. Trying to figure out what one looks like." He grinned.

Rachel playfully responded, "Sorry, you won't find any stereotypes here. It's not like medicine you know, all cut from the same mold. . . ."

"Oh, so you know about these med school types, do you? Personal experience, I presume?" His blue eyes twinkled at the opportunity to tease her.

"Enough of your prying! You'll get nothing out of me." She zipped her lips and threw away a pretend key.

A waiter interrupted to ask about their meal; Rachel asked for another bread stick for Emily and then waved him on.

"So what's your long-range plan with journalism?" Matt asked.

"Oh, I don't know. All depends on job opportunities. I'd really like to be a foreign correspondent though. Or at least national. I could even get into broadcasting. There are so many ways to go."

"Makes my life sound boring in comparison. Guess I'm just following in my father's footsteps . . . and my grandfather's. Never considered being anything but a doctor."

"But you do want to be a doctor, don't you?"

"Yeah, sure. . . ." Matt hesitated slightly. "It's a lot of pressure though. Pressure I could do without."

"So why do you stick with it?"

"You'd have to understand my family. It's important to them, and I don't want to disappoint them."

"What would you do if you weren't going to be a doctor?"

"Hadn't really thought about it. Maybe engineering. I love to figure out how things work. You know, fix things."

"Well, doctors fix things, broken bodies, broken hearts. . . ." She placed her hand over her heart and swooned, "Oh, doctor, save me!"

Matt tried to ignore her theatrics, albeit enchanting. "My Dad thinks I ought to be a surgeon."

"Never mind your father, what do you think?"

"Hey, what's with the third degree?" He winced. "Am I the subject of your next article?"

"You never know." She smiled engagingly.

By now, they were finished with their meal, and little Emily was rubbing her eyes. Matt picked up the bill and looked questioningly at Rachel. "You wanna get some ice cream at Ben and Jerry's?"

"No. Better be going. Got to get Emily to bed; she's exhausted."

"Well, let me walk you out." He followed Rachel to the front, stopping briefly to pay the cashier. Then he hurried to catch up with her as she made her way down Franklin Street.

"Hey, slow down. What's the rush?"

"I just didn't realize it was so late. I have to get Emily down before she loses it."

"Loses it?"

"She's used to a schedule, and if she doesn't get to bed on time, she becomes overtired. Then it's twice as hard to get her to sleep."

"You *act* like this is your daughter."

"Well, I've had plenty of practice. I'm the oldest of four girls, and I can't remember a time when I wasn't playing mommy. This summer I'm working as kind of a nanny. It works out well for me. I keep Emily while Dr. Murdock teaches classes and works on her research, and since I'm only taking one course, most of my time is free to care for Emily."

"You make it seem so easy . . . so natural."

"It is, I guess. Don't you have any brothers and sisters?"

"No. My mother died when I was seven, and my father never remarried."

"I'm sorry."

"Don't be. It's no big deal."

They walked along in silence for a few minutes and then Matt, knowing his out-of-the-ordinary evening was coming to an abrupt end, tried to forestall the inevitable separation. "Hold on, I want to get something for you and Emily." He pulled out his wallet, paid a nearby flower lady for a bunch of daisies, then presented the bowed bouquet to Rachel. "My lady."

Rachel blushed slightly and lowered her eyes. "Thank you. You didn't have to. . . ."

"Oh, but I wanted to. It's not often I get to rescue damsels in distress. It's been my pleasure to serve you."

Rachel repositioned Emily on her hip, took the bouquet, and smiled. "I really do have to go now."

"I understand. But you can't leave until you tell me when I'll see you again."

P r o g e n y

Matt spent the remaining days of his summer internship in Rachel's company—working during the day and then rushing to meet her for dinner. Afterwards, they'd take long, leisurely walks around campus, often joking about how different they were. Rachel would laughingly remind him, "If we were both alike, one of us wouldn't be necessary." But despite their differences, Matt never felt more complete than when he was spending time with Rachel. She added a spontaneity to his life and routinely forced him to break from the rigid work ethic he had developed, long enough to engage a world outside the medical arena.

Once, after pulling an all-nighter, Matt met Rachel at the Carolina Coffee Shop where they all but inhaled an early morning feast of Belgian waffles laden with maple syrup and strawberries. The serene, secluded setting with its classical music wafting eloquently about them, served to magnify their escalating romance and gave no prelude, no hint of an impending clash of ideologies.

It was afterwards, as they strolled arm in arm down Franklin Street past University Church, that Rachel suddenly felt compelled to stop. She pointed towards the massive oak church doors and tugged at Matt's arm. "Hey, it's Sunday. Let's go in."

Matt's reaction was as unexpected as it was callous.

"Absolutely not." He stiffened. "Why would you want to ruin our day like that?"

"That wouldn't ruin our day. How can you say a thing like that?"

"I have no use for church, or God."

"Surely, you don't mean what you're saying."

"I certainly do."

"But why? Why would you be so anti-God?"

"It's not something we need to get into."

"Oh, but it is. It's important for me to understand. Please tell me, help me understand . . . please!" Rachel was insistent.

Matt hesitated, then drew a deep breath. "It's a decision I made when my mother died. I decided I didn't need a God who'd take away a little boy's mother. A God like that wasn't worth my time. Not then, not now."

"But you can't blame God for what happened."

"Why not?"

"You just can't."

"I can. And I did. End of discussion."

"But—"

"But, nothing. I said I don't want to talk about it."

"Oh, Matt, better be careful what you say. One day you'll wake up and realize you need God's love and forgiveness."

"Don't hold your breath."

Progeny

At summer's end, after canoeing around University Lake, Rachel and Matt lounged on a secluded dock and watched the sunset in silence. Then Matt, unable to sit still, got up, gathered some stones and skipped them methodically across the water. After skipping his last rock, he walked back to where Rachel was sitting and stood quietly behind her.

Finally, he opened up, sharing his fears about his upcoming senior year at Hopkins. "I don't know how I'll make it through next year without you around," he began. "Sure, I'll be absorbed in my work, but what will I do without my 'Rachel fixes'?" He knelt down behind her, leaned over her shoulders, and gently pulled back her braided hair, kissing her lightly on the forehead.

Rachel pressed back and wrapped her arms around his muscular legs, then looked up into his eyes. "Well, you know you can visit me anytime. I certainly won't object if you crash my world." Matt fastened his broad hands around her waist and lifted her to a standing position as she continued speaking. "Besides, you'll be back next summer working for Chan, and then you'll start med school in the fall. . . ."

Matt twirled her around to face him. "Ssshh," he whispered, putting his finger to her lips. Then he spoke resolutely, as if he had given a lot of thought to his words. "Making it through next year . . . that will be the test. It will be a sign that we're to make our relationship permanent."

"My, my. Aren't we moving a bit fast?" Rachel quipped, attempting to lighten his serious tone. "Basing decisions on 'signs' isn't the rational Matthew Hamilton I know. Sounds like you're picking up some of my tendencies."

He pulled her close and kissed her softly on the mouth, then declared, "When you know, you know. And I know there's no one I'd rather spend my life with."

Rachel melted in his embrace, buried her face into his chest, and clutched him tightly, savoring the moment. After a bit, she walked over to the edge of the dock, stared out across the lake for what seemed like an eternity, then sat down, and paddled her bare feet in the warm water. Matt was right. She knew there was no one else for her, and she knew she wanted to have his babies. She was as sure of that as she was of her love for him.

The Airport Encounter

CHAPTER 2

15 years later . . .

It was happening again. Drenched in sweat, her heart pounding, Rachel knew it was more than a dream. She didn't dare question its validity. She was an unwitting player, trapped in a nightmarish scenario, and she must react accordingly.

Instinctively, she clutched the child to her breast and ran. Soon they would find her; she knew it. She had no time to reflect, no time to focus on the baby. Was it a girl, a boy? She was the protector. She must find a place to hide.

Surveying the swirling room before her, she knelt down, crawled beneath the massive, wooden desk, and pressed her body against its unyielding mahogany. *Let me be invisible. Please let me disappear.*

In the hushed darkness she made out several towering figures, unrecognizable but formidable. *Who were they, and why were they after her? And just where was she anyway?* Nothing seemed familiar. The flash of a knife's blade prompted another adrenaline surge and effectively halted her questions.

Torn between two worlds—one real, the other illusion—Rachel knew her pursuers were not about to relent. As the footsteps drew closer, she huddled in fright, shielding the child with her body and rocking gently back and forth. All the while, she prayed to elude this enemy, this unknown entity.

Suddenly, the baby cried out, and her hiding place was exposed. The whirlpool intensified, and Rachel felt herself spinning faster and faster. She struggled to hang on to the child, but it was useless; an unexplainable force ripped the child from her grasp and pulled it into the vortex.

Then abruptly, the swirling stopped. The figures faded. Rachel, as if still playing a part, bolted involuntarily to an upright position and pleaded for mercy, "No, no, don't take my baby. Please don't take my baby!"

Sixteen floors down, in the conference room off the main lobby of the Chicago International Hotel, a breakfast seminar was wrapping up. A group of physicians sat perched around tables littered with empty Styrofoam coffee cups, listening intently to Dr. Matt Hamilton sum up his remarks:

"Emotionally troubled children diagnosed with Reactive Attachment Disorder (RAD) have experienced a serious interruption of the bonding cycle during the early stages of life. Although causation is hard to determine, RAD is believed to be caused by pathogenic care from the parent or caregiver. Children with RAD have never learned to trust; become oppositional, angry, and often violently dangerous to themselves and others. If left untreated, these children have the potential for extreme damage, not only to themselves but also to society at large. It is important to remember that intrauterine experience, the mother's attitude, and birth experience all influence the developing bond between mother and child; factors range from overtly traumatic events to emotionally unavailable caregivers. If breaks in the normal bonding process are not identified early on, negative behavior patterns may follow the child well into adult life.

"In closing, I challenge you with this thought: The healthy psychological connectiveness between mother and child remains one of the most fundamental building blocks of human existence. Maintaining this vital foundation is a noble undertaking. We can do no less."

Matt stepped down from the podium as the room full of

psychiatrists broke into applause. He didn't stop to consider the enthusiastic response, just methodically made a getaway toward the side exit. Dr. Art Vaughn caught up with him as he reached the doorway. "So Matt, what's with the great escape?"

"Rachel and I have a plane to catch. I'm cutting it close as it is." Matt quickened his pace, turning towards the elevators.

Vaughn fell in step with the speaker. "Then, I take it you guys aren't sticking around for the big event tonight?" Vaughn referred to the president's banquet—the formal, black-tie conclusion to the weeklong American Academy of Psychiatrists' conference.

"Can't. Gotta get back to Chapel Hill. Told one of the guys I'd take his call."

"Still jumping at every chance to put in more hours, I see. Aren't you ever going to slow down, break the pattern you—we all—developed in residency?"

"Haven't had time to think about it." Matt halted in front of the elevators and hit the up button.

"Why keep pushing yourself so hard? Isn't it enough that you're considered the Academy's 'golden boy'?"

Matt rolled his eyes skeptically.

"No kidding, Matt, this is a big deal. And I for one am truly impressed with your accomplishments."

"Don't be."

"Too late. The damage is done." Vaughn chuckled amicably as he watched Matt step onto the now-open elevator.

Matt smiled tentatively.

"It was good seeing you again."

"You too." Matt offered a parting nod just as the doors closed.

———————

Matt hurried back to the room, mentally checking off his list of things to do. He inserted his passkey and pushed against the door—*resistance!* A fastened security latch stopped him cold, prompting an unjustified surge of aggression. He rattled against the latch, pounding vigorously on the door and bellowing, "Hey, open up!" Bang . . . bang. *"Open up!"*

"Hold on," Rachel's wavering voice called back. "I'm coming." After a short pause, she pulled back the security latch and slowly cracked open the door.

"It's about time," Matt fumed, brushing past her and quickly eyeing the hotel room. "You haven't packed. So predictable." He shook his head out of frustration.

"I had another dream," she said in defense, fingering her short, tousled curls behind her ears. "And I was afraid. I thought something had happened to you."

"Well, I'm fine, and we don't have time to deal with one of your psychotic episodes. Our plane won't wait. Why can't you be ready just once?" He leaned over and began gathering up clothing scattered around the room, stuffing it indelicately into a travel bag.

Pausing momentarily, he faced Rachel again, continuing his barrage. "Move it. Don't you understand plain English?" Inadvertently, he locked onto her eyes—eyes that now registered a faraway look—and for a brief moment remembered why he had married the dark-eyed wisp of a girl standing before him. She was standing helplessly fixated, still dazed, not saying a word. Although his natural tendency was to rescue her, he resisted the unsolicited sense of protectiveness and hastily dismissed his inclination, distancing himself and choosing instead to consider Rachel's irrational behavior.

Her recurring dreams troubled him. The barbiturates should have eliminated the REM sleep cycle completely. And even though he hadn't figured out a way to prevent the dreams entirely, one sleeping pill should have put her into a deep sleep—too deep to dream or at least too deep to remember. But his real concern was why she was dreaming that particular dream. There was no way she could know the truth. Had her unconscious mind recorded the events, in a distorted fashion, leaving only symbolic footprints? It was too eerie for a logical, no-nonsense guy to contemplate. This psychic stuff just didn't compute. Sticking with the facts was easier. Grieving over a lost pregnancy was one thing, but dreaming about someone taking your baby was not a normal grief response, especially for someone who had experienced a "miscarriage."

Music from the radio was the only sound filling the silence during the cab ride to the airport. Rachel knew Matt wasn't mad at her, just annoyed. And she didn't take his criticism as a serious indictment against their relationship, either. They had been together too long not to know what he really meant: "If you cared about what was important to me, you'd make an effort to be on time." She glanced at her watch. She didn't plan to be late, but then, she never did. Matt was *always* on time. Now he was on her case. She hated the pressure.

It had been a rough week. The political side of being chairman of the ethics committee for the American Academy of Psychiatrists had surprised them both. This meeting was no exception. She caught his eyes and gently squeezed his hand. It was those eyes that kept her going. Were they really "bedroom eyes," as an OR nurse once remarked during a surgery rotation? Granted, they were captivating, steel blue and all you could see behind the mask. The nurse's comments were understandable; combining those seductive eyes with his muscular, six-foot frame produced a tempting package. But whether the nurse's remark was meant to elicit a sexual response mattered little, as Matt's attention seldom deviated from his medical responsibilities. Rachel was surprised he remembered the comment long enough to tell her about it that evening years ago.

James Taylor's melancholy "Fire and Rain" played softly in the background as Rachel's thoughts drifted back to medical school and residency. Those years had been tough for both of them, but it was the miscarriage during med school that had taken the greatest toll on their marriage. Even now, fifteen years later, the pain still lingered. The anniversary of that first miscarriage, December 12, was fast approaching, and Rachel dreaded the memories it evoked.

Although she conceived without difficulty—that time and five times thereafter—the problem was holding onto the pregnancies. Her body simply did not cooperate with the planned program. At least the memory of the first time, unmarred by the anxiety and uncertainties accompanying later conceptions, provided some degree of comfort.

As was typical for a first pregnancy, Rachel had envisioned what it would be like to have a baby around—her baby. She even tried on the mother role by caring for a neighbor's newborn. Little Caleb would wrap his tiny fingers around hers, clenching tightly; and when she held him, he quieted instantly. Rachel interpreted the flood of maternal feelings accompanying that one small act as a sign that motherhood would somehow complete her. When she became pregnant, she shared her excitement with everyone, sparing no one the news. She bought baby clothes (steering clear of blues or pinks) and even wore maternity clothes before she was "showing." Then there was the rocker—a flea market bargain—providing a day-to-day reminder that soon she would be a mother.

Matt, on the other hand, did not voice any feelings over the matter, nor did he display any positive emotions. Rachel resorted to her usual habit of reading his thoughts as best she could. Practically, the timing was off. Matt was in his first year of medical school. Money was a big issue; space was at a premium.

The cab took a quick left, throwing the couple off balance. Although aggressive, the cabbie possessed a self-confidence that came with years of experience, and Chicago traffic was no match for him. The snow was falling lightly, and impatient drivers, aggravated with the sudden change in weather conditions, foolishly wove in and out of traffic, passing slow-moving vehicles with reckless abandon. It was only a matter of time before someone wrecked. Rachel and Matt didn't seem to notice; they were too absorbed in their thoughts.

———————

Chaos reigned at O'Hare. Matt and Rachel's cab eased up to the curb, edging out the competitors. "We don't have much time," Matt announced, paying the cabbie and grabbing three of the four bags. Rachel, responsible for the carry-on, watched as Matt struggled to maintain his balance. Of course, he would never ask for help. Paying five dollars to a skycap would not only be an admission of defeat but would also make him dependent upon someone else. Arguing with him about his senseless behavior was useless; Rachel didn't even bother commenting. She pulled out her ticket and reviewed the flight schedule while trying to keep up with Matt's frenzied pace.

"We've got at least an hour wait," Rachel chided. "I can't believe we rushed; look what time it is." Rachel held out her watch as proof.

"By the time we check our baggage and find the gate, it'll be time to board," Matt responded. "Besides, we have to get to another terminal; they've already changed gates on us." Matt pointed to the departure schedules flashing on the overhead screens.

The check-in line was inching along; moving slower than the grocery store check-out line at 5:00 P.M. Matt was not pleased. *If they missed their flight,* Rachel thought, *of course, it would be her fault.* Matt's disapproving look, shot her way while they waited to go through the security checkpoint, was confirmation. But surely he couldn't blame her for tightened security measures and the extra time required for checking in? Last summer's airline explosion was the culprit responsible for that.

Then it happened. Not the best timing for an earth-shattering revelation, but nevertheless it happened. Rachel had already gone through the metal detector and was waiting for Matt to retrieve his keys and loose change from the plastic basket. Glancing through the glass partition into the adjacent corridor, Rachel noticed a girls' athletic team: several schoolgirls, all dressed alike in warm-up suits, probably around fifteen years old. They were walking towards Rachel, giggling and pointing to some older guys in front of them. *Must have been a regional or national game to get to fly.*

Suddenly, a girl with long, auburn hair turned in Rachel's direction and for one brief moment, they locked eyes. Time froze. It was as if Rachel had gone back in time and was staring into a mirror. The girl was an exact portrait of herself at that age. Past memories paraded across her mind's eye like a home movie. It was an unsettling experience.

Startled by Rachel's stare, the girl quickly looked away and nonchalantly resumed her conversation, seemingly unaffected by the encounter. Rachel, on the other hand, did not react so calmly. She stood transfixed, watching the girl intently. Something significant had just occurred. Something of cosmic proportions. It wasn't just the resemblance. It was something more. There was something about the girl that connected them; a mystical bond she couldn't explain. She felt it. Intuitively, she knew it.

"You look like you've just seen a ghost," Matt said, disrupting the magic of the moment. Then, not waiting for a response, quickly added, "Let's go."

"I can't," Rachel stammered, "I—we've got to follow those kids," pointing to the group disappearing around the corner. She turned and started in their direction, but Matt grabbed her arm.

"What, are you crazy? Our plane is about to take off."

"Matt, you're not going to believe this, but I just saw . . . I just saw a girl who could be my . . . my daughter."

"You're right, I'm not going to believe it," he tightened his grip and pulled her along toward their gate.

Rachel didn't resist. Confused and shaken, she acquiesced. Let Matt have his way. She needed time to sort through what she had just seen. It was too vivid to be a fantasy. Those were real kids, in real uniforms, coming back from a real trip. But how could the girl look so much like her? It defied logic.

The loudspeaker blared as they approached the gate, "This is the final call for Flight 1209 to Raleigh-Durham."

"Just in time," Matt breathed as he hastened through the doorway to the plane, still clutching Rachel's arm.

Liftoff was a blur. Rachel was seated in the window seat, her mind still focused on the girl. She mentally clicked the familiar face into her memory—same dark eyes, same little turned-up nose—and made a concentrated effort to remember details of the school group. Then she considered Matt's lack of reaction. Logically, of course, why should he? There was no chance the child could be hers, was there? Still, something was wrong, and Matt hadn't even seemed interested in pursuing it. How typical. Ignore it, maybe it will go away. That was Matt's philosophy, and it made her angry, but she knew bringing up the subject again would only provoke further disbelief. He would just treat the encounter like he treated her dreams: all in her mind. One more reason to think she was going over the edge.

———————

"I think you need to be on Haldol," Matt announced, breaking a two-hour silence. It was his first comment since they had boarded, and it effectively halted Rachel's in-flight inspection of the terrain as they flew over Chapel Hill on their approach to RDU airport.

"What?" Rachel said without turning from the window.

"I said, 'I think you should be on Haldol.'" Matt impatiently repeated himself.

Rachel slowly turned from the window with a quizzical look. "Haldol? What are you talking about?"

"The sighting back in Chicago. Your mind is playing tricks on you. Probably related to your dream earlier this morning."

"Matt! There was no trick to it. What I saw was real."

"I know you think it was real, but trust me, your mind is capable of this, especially considering the state you're in."

"State? What state? Matthew Hamilton, I'm not crazy. How many times do I have to tell you?"

"Rachel! Calm down. I didn't say you were crazy . . . confused maybe . . . not crazy. There's a difference, you know."

"Believe me, I know the difference. Enough of your analysis already."

"Hey, your dreams are a dead giveaway. You're obviously still harboring guilt over being childless, and now it's crossing over and distorting reality. That's why you need to be on Haldol. It'll inhibit any hallucinations or delusional thinking."

"But I'm not imagining this. And another drug is the last thing I need."

"The way I see it, we really don't have a choice. The situation is only going to get worse if we don't address it now. Drug therapy would be my recommendation for anyone with your symptoms."

"Matt, you're always so negative. Always expecting the worst to happen. Why rush into this?"

"Because it's necessary. And besides, we wouldn't be dealing with this problem if you'd taken your sleeping pills like I told you to."

"Wait just a minute. Don't start in on me as if I'm to blame. I haven't had a dream like that in a long time. I thought they were over. Why keep popping pills if I don't need them? Besides, I don't like the effect they have on me."

"Rachel, you have to do what I say if you're going to beat this thing. You know that. Hopefully, the Haldol will help. If you're not having paranoid delusions, then maybe the dreams will stop."

As always, Matt was quite convincing, and Rachel seriously considered the possibility that the airport encounter may have been a figment of her imagination. The prospect was frightening. If anything, the dreams had taught her that there was a fine line between reality and fantasy, but it was hard to believe her mind could actually trick her into thinking she had seen the look-alike girl. Was Matt right in his assessment? Was she really crazy?

"You really . . . really think I'm delusional, don't you?"

"What else? Look at the content of your dreams," Matt answered confidently.

"But couldn't they be based on something real?"

"I'm not getting into this with you again." Matt immediately dismissed her question, displaying the "don't push me further" look which Rachel recognized all too well.

Disregarding the warning, she pressed her point further. "But I did an Internet search on dreams, and the article I read said that lucid dreams were trying to tell you something. Something your conscious mind has rejected."

"Rachel, forget it." Matt said firmly, ending the conversation. "We've been through this a thousand times. Accept the facts. It's nothing. The sooner you get that out of your mind, the better off you'll be. Trust me."

CHAPTER 3

Chicago Revisited

The sun was setting when Rachel and Matt arrived home from Chicago. Although still somewhat confused and shaken by the airport encounter earlier that day, Rachel wasted no time in beginning her quest. By 6:00 P.M., she was seated at her tiny desk at the Chapel Hill News, surfing the Internet for answers. She was determined to find some record, some article, some photo, that would convince Matt she wasn't hallucinating about the girl she saw in the airport. Since she had completed her assignment on tightened security measures at the Raleigh-Durham airport before their trip, Rachel was free to concentrate on finding information about the Chicago girls' team. She wasn't about to allow Matt to categorize the mysterious encounter as a delusion. She had to prove her case. That was the only way he would take her seriously. The only way he'd quit pushing her to take Haldol.

Glued to her computer terminal, Rachel settled into her confined space among the other desks crowded into the main newsroom of the small weekly paper. A long night was ahead of her. There were two major newspapers in the Chicago area, the *Chicago Tribune* and the *Chicago Sun-Times,* as well as scores of small-town papers. Pulling up sports-related articles was an endless task and with the Bulls dominating the scene, the search soon took its toll. Rachel decided to take a break and refill her coffee mug.

The coffee room was empty, and the only sign of life was an overhead light flickering on and off. Rachel pulled out a cheap, plastic chair from around the table, sat down, and sipped her coffee in solitude. Finally, sufficiently annoyed by the flickering light and unable to understand why no one had taken the time to screw the bulb in tighter, Rachel slipped off her clogs and climbed onto the chair, attempting to steady herself as she reached toward the single bulb. *This isn't going to work.* She stepped up onto the Formica-topped table and teetered on tiptoes as she stretched upward once more.

"OUCH!" The bulb was too hot to handle even with a dish towel, and Rachel flinched in pain. Suddenly she lost her footing and fell—only to be caught by the paper's ready and willing photographer.

"Scott! Where did you come from?" a startled Rachel cried out.

"I just happened to be walking by when I saw this voluptuous figure reaching for the heavens. Thought it was an angel preparing for flight."

Rachel struggled to free herself from Scott's herculean arms.

Scott frowned but let her go. "Just trying to help."

"Hey, if you want to be helpful, you can fix that light," Rachel asserted, pointing upward. "And if you really want to score points, you can help me look through sports photos on the Internet."

"Anything for a little attention," he winked.

"Scott!" Rachel shot him a menacing look.

"OK, OK. No harm in trying. . . . So what exactly are you looking for?"

The predawn conversation was going nowhere, and Matt didn't try to hide his irritation. It was just too early in the morning to deal with Rachel's compulsive behavior. "Look at the dark circles under your eyes. Why, you didn't even sleep last night, did you?" Matt groaned, shaking his head in disbelief. "You're obsessed with this thing."

"I know you think I'm crazy, but it's true," Rachel snapped. "Besides, why would I invent a phantom daughter?" She waved a copy of an Associated Press wire photo in his face.

"You tell me," Matt replied calmly, raising his eyebrows and ignoring the photo.

"Knock off the psychoanalysis. I hate it when you treat me like one of your patients." Rachel pushed her chair away from the kitchen table, stood up, and walked over to the coffeepot, intent on avoiding Matt's gaze. She couldn't stand to face him when he talked to her like that.

"Then tell me how I'm supposed to act when my wife comes up with this incredibly unbelievable story?" Matt was becoming increasingly sarcastic. "'Gee, my wife saw our daughter today. Of course, we both know we don't have a daughter. We both know she's never even given birth.' This is ridiculous! Why am I even having this conversation?"

Rachel turned back towards him and forcefully responded, "Because it's true. And you have to help me figure it out."

"There's nothing to figure out. Just drop it." Matt got up from his chair, sat his coffee mug down on the counter next to Rachel and announced, "I've got an office meeting. Gotta go." He gave her a perfunctory kiss on the cheek, then turned and disappeared out the back door.

Rachel slumped down in the Windsor chair next to the bay window. *I have to get to the bottom of this. I have to find that mystery girl.*

"Anyone home?" A familiar voice broke the silence.

"Oh, Jenny. Good. Come in." Rachel crossed the room to greet her neighbor who was standing in the open door-way. She gave the woman a hello hug and then shut the door behind her. Jenny Sanderson was a great friend, having bonded immediately with Rachel when the Hamiltons first moved into the neighborhood five years earlier.

"I wasn't sure you'd be back from your trip, but I took a chance." Jenny, dressed in her designer sweats, gasped for air and then dropped into the nearest chair. "I couldn't make it around the block one more time. I'm exhausted. This new exercise program better work." She continued rambling, "If I don't lose twenty pounds in two months, I'm getting my money back. I've bought new sweats and everything." She stood up and twirled around to model her outfit.

"I'm glad you're here. I really need your help." Rachel changed the subject, her mind still focused on Matt's skepti-cism.

"Hey, relax, don't look so intense. Did you and Matt have another fight? He did seem a little agitated on his way out."

"I know," Rachel moaned. "Same old story. We never

finish a conversation, never resolve anything. It's pretty bad when your own husband won't believe you."

Jenny straightened up and nodded sympathetically. "So what's the problem *this* time?"

"Let me fix some tea first. You need to be in the right frame of mind to hear this one." Rachel purposely stopped the flow of the conversation. She was intent on convincing Jenny and knew she needed to present her speculations carefully, especially after Matt had summarily dismissed them.

"Go throw another log on the fire for me." Rachel ordered, waving Jenny into the living room. "I'll be there in a minute."

"Sure. I always like being waited on. . . ."

Chamomile was Jenny's favorite tea, but finding the box of tea bags was going to be a chore. None of Rachel's groceries ever ended up in the same place, since she crammed everything—cans of pineapple, refried beans, pasta, brown rice, herbal teas—on the shelves wherever there was room. She had no organized system and always told Matt it was because she didn't have enough cabinet space. Whether that was an accurate assessment or a moot point, Rachel loved her house and was not about to move simply to acquire a bigger kitchen. Years of living in married student housing with its cinder block walls created a strong incentive for more aesthetically pleasing quarters, so when Matt agreed to stay on as faculty after completing his fellowship at Carolina, he and Rachel began a diligent search for the perfect home. The charming Cape Cod nestled among the trees easily qualified. Matt liked the front porch. Rachel loved the small, cozy rooms with hardwood floors and considered the glass door-knobs a fringe benefit. In time, oriental rugs and over-stuffed chairs filled the living room.

The teakettle whistled. Rachel found the tea bags, poured hot water over them, and then performed her balancing act. She placed a folder under her arm, clutched the mugs, ducked beneath the overhanging pot rack, and carefully made her way out to the living room without spilling a drop.

"You have to trust me on this one," Rachel began as she curled up in the chair opposite Jenny. "But promise you won't think I'm wacko?"

"I think I can handle it."

"But this is going to sound off the wall. Really off the wall. Promise me."

"OK, promise. Now tell me."

"In the airport coming home, I saw a girl—a girl I think I am connected to in some strange way. It's weird. She looks like me." Rachel spit the last part out.

"So? Lots of people look alike." Jenny didn't get her point.

"No." Rachel was insistent. "This girl could have been me. It's not just a 'look alike,' it's like . . . my flesh and blood." There, she'd said it. "Call it a hunch, call it whatever you like, but you know my psychic sense is usually right."

Ready to defend her assertion, Rachel braced herself for the doubts and the outright disbelief. She held her breath and closely monitored Jenny's expression.

Bewildered, Jenny sat quietly, carefully weighing Rachel's words—words that were definitely hard to swallow but spoken convincingly, nevertheless. No doubt she was serious. Jenny knew about Rachel's past, littered with failed pregnancies and knew how desperate she was to have a child. "It doesn't make sense, but if you need my help, I'm in," Jenny finally responded, trying to camouflage her doubts.

Rachel sighed gratefully. "I spent all last night going through old family photos. Check this one out." Rachel handed Jenny a picture from her folder. "You have to help me find this girl . . . or one that looks like this."

Jenny looked intently at the photo of a teenage Rachel: a slender, dark-haired beauty with captivating eyes. "How much did you weigh back then anyway?"

"About 110."

"Well, it's definitely you, except maybe for a few more pounds and short hair." Jenny chuckled. "I wish someone could recognize me from my high-school picture."

"Get serious."

"I am, I am. But it's not like you're asking for the moon or anything. Do you realize that if anyone else heard this conversation, they'd think we were nuts? You, for thinking you saw a daughter you never had and me for even talking to you about it." She sat back and laughed, "We are nuts."

"Let 'em think I'm nuts, even Matt, but I'm going to find this girl," Rachel said with unflinching resolve. "I've already started searching for her school." Rachel stopped momentarily, retrieving a clipping from her pile of papers. "I found this article and photo from the sports page of the *Chicago Tribune* when I was surfing the net." She reached over and handed the clipping to Jenny. The photo caption read: "Coach Terrell Congratulates Captain Wendy Jamison." Jenny gave the article a quick review and then looked questioningly at Rachel.

"This picture would have meant nothing before the airport incident," Rachel explained. "But this is the same group. Look," Rachel said triumphantly "the jackets, are the same."

"Don't you think other teams have these same jackets?" Jenny asked hesitantly.

"Sure, but what other teams recently won a tournament and were in the airport—coming home—the day after their win? This is the same team. I know it."

"OK, this may be the team you saw, but how does it help find the girl?"

"We call the school and ask for a roster of players."

"Right," Jenny interjected with a tinge of doubt in her voice. "Like they're going to give information over the phone to a stranger."

"Just pretend you're doing a follow-up story on Midland Prep's big win."

"Wait a minute. Since when did *I* become the investigative reporter? I'm the speech pathologist, remember? And what good will a roster do anyway? You don't even know the girl's name? Give it up, Rachel, this isn't working."

"There must be a way. Think."

"You don't know her name. No one's going to give you her name. You'll have to go in person to find her. That's the only way it'll work."

———————

Rachel fastened her seat belt, ignored the flight instructions droning over the speaker, and reviewed her plan of action: arrive in Chicago, rent a car, get a map, and drive straight to Midland Prep. It had been a hassle setting up the trip to Chicago without Matt knowing, and although she wanted to tell him, Rachel knew it would have to wait until she had some solid evidence, something more convincing than a team photo from the Internet. Besides, she didn't want to hear his protests.

As always, Jenny was her partner in crime, driving her to the airport once Matt left for work and promising to cover for her while she was away. Since it was just a day trip, Rachel was confident her husband wouldn't even miss her. The main objective was to get a picture of the girl, something tangible for Matt to see. If she could just find out if the girl was adopted or related in some distant way—maybe that would explain the resemblance. The plan seemed easy enough. Then surely he would help get to the bottom of the mystery.

Approximately two hours later, Rachel found herself behind the wheel of a white Ford Taurus heading southwest. The traffic was heavy, but at least she had missed rush hour— the result of good planning. The Chicago phone book had listed Midland Prep in Downers Grove. The map gave a general overview but offered no specifics. She would just have to ask for directions when she got there. After nearly an hour of hits and misses, she finally pulled up in front of a large stone building. "Midland Preparatory Academy, Founded 1952." Rachel briefly perused the engraving chiseled in the stone facade and then scurried through the main doors, relieved to leave the chilling cold behind. Her long wool coat had been a must for this trip, although it provided little protection from the wind whipping around her ears. The lobby was as impressive as it was massive. Marble flooring and solid wood paneling lent an aristocratic air. The open stairwell led her eyes upward to the high, vaulted ceiling.

Camera and small notebook in hand, Rachel pulled herself together, mentally assumed the role of reporter, and marched assertively into an office across the hallway. She approached a lady standing behind the counter. Smiling broadly, she began reciting her prepared script. "Hi. I'm looking for Coach Terrell. I'm doing a follow-up story on Midland Prep's big win."

"I'm sorry. He's not in."

"Oh, well . . . perhaps I could arrange to take a picture of the team during practice today?"

"There's no soccer practice today." The lady was not very helpful and offered no alternatives.

"I'll need to check with my editor to see about rescheduling. May I use your phone?" Rachel didn't have anyone to call, but she needed time to think. She couldn't just leave. Gripped by a sense of desperation, the "plan" began to unravel in her mind. *Stay cool,* she told herself, *don't panic.* She couldn't give in to the fear. She had to remain professional . . . even if her palms were clammy and she felt flushed and weak. Then, almost instinctively, she did something she hadn't done in years: She shot an arrow prayer upward, "Please help."

The receptionist interrupted her thoughts and motioned toward the phone on a nearby desk, "Use that one."

"Thanks." Grateful for the momentary diversion, Rachel dialed several numbers and faked listening for a reply. Then, while standing there, she noticed a school newspaper lying open, a soccer team photo in full view. "Oh, my," she gasped aloud, surprised by the rapid answer to her prayer. The lady's beady eyes bored a hole right through her, and Rachel weakly offered an apologetic look. She hadn't been reprimanded for speaking out loud in quite a while, and this wasn't even a library.

As Rachel continued her pretend phone conversation, her eyes scanned the school paper for names and faces. There . . . there she was. The girl! She fought hard to contain her excitement. Discreetly, she picked up the newspaper and folded it beneath her notebook. She hung up the phone. Then, with careful deliberation, she looked straight into the woman's face. "I need the phone numbers of several girls to arrange interviews, perhaps we can start with Elise Prescott." The unfamiliar name sounded awkward coming from her lips.

"Elise!" The woman shrilled, a horrified look plastered on her face. "Dr. Prescott would never allow that."

Realizing she had pushed the wrong button, Rachel knew the charade was over. Immediately, the woman regained her composure, assumed a mechanical posture, and walked quickly towards Rachel. "You'll have to leave now. Our policy strictly forbids giving out such information." The woman took Rachel firmly by the arm, escorted her through the office door, and curtly ended their exchange. "Good day!"

Dutifully, Rachel made her way towards the front entrance, sensing the woman's glare following her. It was noon, and the previously empty halls were now jammed with students. Rachel glanced over her shoulder and noticed the office lady momentarily preoccupied with another woman. She seized the opportunity and quickly slipped unnoticed into the flow of the crowd, intent upon accomplishing her mission. Following the boys and girls into the cafeteria, Rachel tried to blend in. She approached a group of kids waiting in a food line, stood behind the last guy and began her questioning. "Where could I find Elise Prescott?"

The tall, skinny boy with a case of severe acne answered flatly, "With the soccer team, most likely."

"And that would be . . . where?" Rachel waited for his reply.

"Round table near the windows." The boy begrudgingly pointed toward a group of girls congregating across the room.

"Thanks." Rachel turned and headed in that direction, her heart beating rapidly. As she approached the table, she searched through the group, hoping to identify Elise. *I knew this was too easy. She's not going to be here.*

"Hi," Rachel said, seating herself amid the chattering girls. "I'm looking for Elise Prescott."

Immediately, the group fell silent. Then one girl, dressed in a plaid jumper with matching tights, asked suspiciously, "Why do you want her?"

"I saw her in the airport, and I'm just trying to find her."

"You're the lady from the airport?" the girl blurted out.

"You know about that?" Rachel replied in wide-eyed amazement.

"We all know," the girl announced. "Elise was freaked out. A strange woman staring at her and all." All the girls nodded in agreement.

"It wasn't like that. I wasn't trying to frighten anyone," Rachel attempted to allay the girl's suspicions. "I just thought she looked like me. It was curiosity. Nothing more."

"Well, you really did a number on Elise. She talked about it all the way home from the airport," another girl chimed in, closely eyeing Rachel. "You do look a lot alike though."

"Where . . . where is Elise?" Rachel asked hesitantly, afraid the answer would disappoint her.

"Latin club field trip."

"When will she be back?"

"Late tonight."

"Great." Rachel moaned, dropping her head into her hands.

"What do you want with her?"

"I just wanted to talk, maybe get a picture. Maybe I should talk with her parents," Rachel mumbled, thinking out loud.

"I wouldn't try that," the first girl warned.

"What's wrong with talking to her parents? What's everyone so afraid of?" Rachel queried, remembering the office lady's peculiar reaction.

"Her parents are weird," a soft-spoken girl offered. "No one likes to go over there. Dr. and Mrs. Prescott won't let her do anything or go anywhere with her friends. They treat her like she's a trophy or something. Elise once told me that she thought she was adopted."

"Is she?" Rachel asked.

"I don't know. But she doesn't fit in with them. She's not like them at all. I feel sorry for her."

"And she sure doesn't look like her mother!" A cute, freckle-faced pixie piped in. The girls started giggling as if sharing an inside joke.

"Uh-oh," one of the girls sounded the alarm. "Here

comes Mrs. Haggar." All eyes turned toward a woman barreling toward them.

Rachel recognized the woman from the office. "Guess I better be going," she said, slipping out of her seat and proceeding to the nearest exit.

The windchill factor registered 15 degrees below zero. Huddled and shivering before the open phone booth, Rachel tried unsuccessfully to block out the gusts of wind whipping around her face. Forced to take off her gloves to thumb through the residential pages of the tattered phone book, her fingers were numb by the time she finally found the listing. Time was closing in. She knew she had to catch her return flight, but surely she could find 1123 Idlewild Boulevard first. . . .

CHAPTER 4

Critical Mass

Matt was dictating notes on his last patient when the phone began ringing. It rang at least six times before he realized the office staff had left an hour ago. Reaching over, he picked up the receiver and glanced at the wall clock: 6:15.

"Hello."

"This is the Downers Grove Police Department. I need

to speak with a Dr. Matthew Hamilton."

"This is he."

"I have a woman here who claims to be your wife, a Rachel Duncan Hamilton."

"That's my wife's name, but she's at home."

"Can you verify that?"

"Sure, let me call my house."

"Wait a minute," the officer paused a moment. "The young lady would like to speak with you."

"Matt?" a trembling voice said.

"Rachel!"

"Please don't be mad. It was something I had to do."

"What are you talking about? Where are you?"

"Chicago. I tracked the airport girl down."

Matt swore under his breath, then lashed out, "You've really done it now, Rachel!"

"Don't act like that. She's real, just like I said."

"Did you see her?"

"Well, no, but. . . ."

"But nothing. Rachel, you can't go chasing delusions. Other people won't understand . . . other people don't understand!"

"I know, you'll have to explain it to them."

"I'm not explaining anything."

"Will you at least tell these guys I'm your wife, so they'll believe me?"

"That I can do. Let me talk to the officer."

The gruff voice resumed. "This is Officer Davidson again. Was that your wife?"

"Yes. Could you please tell me what's going on?"

"Seems the little lady created quite a ruckus at the Prescott home late this afternoon."

"Prescott?"

"Yes, Dr. Forrest Prescott, pretty important fella around these parts. Head of Biotech, the big research facility."

"Could you start at the beginning?"

"Be glad to. Your wife somehow bypassed the security guards and trespassed onto Prescott's estate. Harassed Prescott and his wife—something about looking for her daughter."

"I can't believe this," Matt mumbled, more to himself than the officer.

"Well, you better believe it and hope Prescott doesn't press charges. He's a stickler about his privacy."

"Can my wife come home now?"

"That'll be up to the commissioner."

"The commissioner?"

"Yeah, that's the way it works. We process her through our system, then she goes before the commissioner. He determines whether she can be released on her own recognizance or if she'll have to post bail."

"You think he'll let her go?"

"There's no record, so I suspect so. But whichever way it goes, let me give you a little friendly advice: From now on, keep the little lady in your neck of the woods."

"No problem. Is there something I should do? Like maybe catch a plane up there?"

"I don't think that's necessary. Better just sit tight and wait for her to call."

Matt tried to concentrate on the ethics report on his desk but couldn't. He stretched and leaned back in his chair, closing his eyes as he replayed the events of the day. He didn't like being reminded of Rachel's obsessions. They always provoked feelings of guilt—guilt he made a point of rationalizing away even though he knew deep down that their marriage wouldn't be falling apart and Rachel wouldn't be on the verge of a mental breakdown if he'd been stronger, less self-absorbed. He often tried to assure himself that Rachel's failure to carry a child to term was a physiological problem, not the result of his actions. But he knew all too well the theories attributing early pregnancy loss to psychological factors and knew that stress undeniably triggered a chemical reaction which released prostaglandins into the bloodstream. Unless stopped, prostaglandins initiated the sequence starting labor. Nevertheless, he convinced himself, he couldn't be held responsible for Rachel's psychological state.

After the first "miscarriage," Matt had escaped into his medical world, insulating himself from the truth and sustaining his denial of what had really happened. Most of the time, his defense system worked well. However, he had never been completely able to escape the sick feeling in the pit of his stomach each time he remembered. Usually he could block the whole incident out of his mind, but this evening's phone call unleashed a flood of memories. In particular, a conversation he'd had with Dr. Chan fifteen years earlier.

Newly married, Matt was juggling med school and working in Chan's lab between semesters, during vacations, whenever he found the time. Rachel was carrying his child. She was overtly happy. He was internally conflicted. She wasn't concerned about the future—how a child would affect their lives. And she found no difficulty combining motherhood with completing her journalism degree. "No problem," she'd say confidently. "Why shouldn't I be able to finish and have a baby, too?" He never responded to her idealism. He just knew she wasn't grounded in reality. For him, the realism of having a child at that point in their lives was too heavy to bear.

Dr. Chan, the cold and methodical researcher, seemed bewildered over the predicament one day when Matt mentioned the problem. "Where my people come from," he instructed, "one would abort the child without question. In fact, the state would applaud such a rational decision."

"That's easy for you to say, but she's five months along." Matt defended his reluctance.

"That's not a problem. Abortion is possible at any stage of pregnancy. Something the privileged have come to depend on."

"Not in America."

"Don't be so naïve, Matt. Money is a powerful incentive."

"Well, it doesn't matter. Rachel would never agree."

"She wouldn't have to know."

Such a bold assertion startled Matt. This man can't be serious, he thought. "OK, I'll bite. Tell me how I could pull that off."

"I've been experimenting with mifepristone, a drug that if ingested, will cause the fetus to detach from the womb. Combine that with prostaglandins, and you can simulate a spontaneous abortion—ah, 'miscarriage' if you prefer." Chan chortled under his breath. "You Americans . . . always trying to soften reality with the choice of your words." He shook his head in disbelief and continued. "The problem is then with the uterine contents. Although no longer viable, they must be extracted."

Feeling increasingly uncomfortable with the discussion but still curious, Matt interrupted Chan's mini-lecture. "What do you mean, Rachel wouldn't have to know."

"Patience. Have her visit me for a normal obstetrical exam. Tell her you want the best possible care. I'll take care of the rest."

"You talk as if this happens all the time."

"Maybe it does."

Matt felt himself being pulled involuntarily into a malevolent vortex, and although his first instinct was to bolt, his intrigue held him steady. "You'd never get Rachel to take an experimental drug. She isn't a pushover."

"But when she sees the tissue I remove during the exam, she'll believe she's about to miscarry. Then she'll willingly take anything I prescribe to sustain the pregnancy. Which, of course, won't actually sustain anything."

Matt was speechless. Just how did someone respond to such a devious scheme? How could Chan act so matter-of-fact, so coldhearted? *My God,* Matt thought, *what have I stumbled into?*

As if reading his thoughts, Chan offered his assistance. "Let me make it easy for you. All you have to do is bring her here when the contractions become unbearable. I'll handle the rest!"

Tripping over his words, Matt tried to back out of the conversation, "I, I don't think this is the right solution for us. . . ."

Chan wasn't about to let go. "Let's examine the circumstances. You have at least seven more years of medical training ahead. Add to that a couple of extra years, depending on the specialty you choose. Then there are the loans you have to repay for your undergraduate education. How are you going to pay for all of that with a wife and baby to support? The way I see it, you don't have a choice."

Matt tried to focus on Rachel and her disappointment but couldn't. His father's prior warning haunted him. He could see the stern expression and hear the harsh, patriarchal words echoing in his mind as if it were yesterday, "You marry that girl and I promise you, you'll never finish your training. And don't even think about asking for money. You won't get a cent from me!" Had his father been right?

Matt stared at the wall phone hanging next to the lab

entrance and considered how his father never bothered to return his calls. It was deliberate; his father would never give in, never renege on his ultimatum. As far as the elder Dr. Hamilton was concerned, Matt was formally disinherited. He expected Matt to fail, even predicted it. Now he was waiting in the wings to blame Rachel when it happened. Matt couldn't let that happen. Not now, not ever. . . .

Chan's persuasive assault jolted Matt back into the picture. "My partners are willing to make this proposition well worth your efforts."

"Partners, what partners? Who in their right mind would pay for this disgusting arrangement?"

"You'd be surprised," Chan replied. "My colleagues place a high value on fetal tissue and are willing to pay top dollar. Do some research on your own. Then you'll understand. It's quite a profitable business. The going rate is $5,000."

A wave of panic washed over Matt, and he thought he would lose his lunch. Chan's argument made sense. Money *was* an issue. Matt felt his resistance eroding, and any moral courage he may have possessed was quickly draining away.

In a sick, fatherly way Chan put his arm around Matt and walked him to the door. He handed him his business card and advised, "Give this to your wife. Tell her I'm expecting her call. . . ."

"Beep, beep, beep." Matt's pager jarred him awake, and he found himself slumped down in the leather chair where he'd been trying to read the ethics committee's report. He pulled himself up, leaned over, and read the number on the pager display. Hmmm. Not a hospital number. Then he remembered Rachel.

He dialed the number and waited for a response.

"Hello, Matt?"

"Figured it was you."

"I'm at the airport. Can you come get me?"

"Be there in a minute." Matt offered no words of welcome, no terms of endearment. The current situation did not please him. His relationship with Rachel was at critical mass. Thoughts were racing as he made his way out the door. *How can this be happening? Things have gotten way out of control. Time to reevaluate.* Matt knew he needed a plan to divert Rachel's attention away from her obsession with the girl in Chicago. Maybe, just maybe, it was time to get serious about having a child. The idea appealed to him. Besides, he had been on faculty for five years now and felt secure in that position. The timing was right.

The other issue was whether to take her off the drugs. Would she be stable? It was a chance he would have to take. And the dreams? Without a disrupted REM cycle induced by the barbiturates, the dreams were sure to return. Hopefully they would last only until a baby was born. Listening to Rachel reiterate her dreams was difficult, if not intolerable.

P r o g e n y

The traces of truth unnerved him, but he was determined to get past the pathology that had held him captive for fifteen years and was now destroying his marriage. Captive to a lie. Captive to deception. He was a slave, and he wanted his freedom. He wished he had never met Chan. Moreover, he wished he hadn't been so afraid of having a baby . . . so consumed with his own plans that there was no room for a child.

The landing gear lights lit up the sky. Planes never seemed as big as when they came in for landings over the interstate. This one flew right over Matt's late-model Scout, a vehicle he found quite suitable even though it didn't qualify as a status symbol. He braced himself for his rendezvous with Rachel. It wasn't under the most pleasant of circumstances, and he needed to get his thoughts in order before picking her up.

By the time he reached the baggage claim area, it was drizzling rain. Matt spotted his wife between swipes of the windshield wipers—standing alone, waiting patiently in her long, red wool coat. For one solitary moment, it struck Matt that he hadn't really "seen" her in quite a while. Yes, she was the same woman he had married, still a knockout after all the years. Her looks could have attracted many men, yet she seemed content with him. He'd never understood that.

He pulled up close enough for her to jump in, close enough to see that she was a disheveled mess and that her lower lip was quivering uncontrollably. As she looked up and met his eyes, Rachel immediately dissolved into tears.

"I'm so sorry, I'm so sorry." She blurted out between sobs as she plopped in the front seat. "I can't get past this! What's wrong with me?"

Matt ignored her question. An airport terminal was just not the appropriate place for that conversation. "I plan on discussing this with you," he began, "but not here, not now."

Rachel was weeping openly. She had completely lost control. "Why can't I be like normal people?"

"It looks like I don't have a choice," Matt mumbled to himself, realizing the timing couldn't be altered. He drove a little further and then pulled off on the side of the road. Turning to face her, he began speaking. "What in the world were you thinking going to Prescott's house?"

Rachel didn't respond.

"I said, 'What were you thinking?'" Matt's words shot out forcefully, but Rachel was huddled against the car door crying uncontrollably now, giving no indication that she heard him. This disarmed Matt. He wasn't accustomed to having his directives ignored. He paused to study his wife— a mass of raw emotion. *How could two people bound together in the most intimate of relationships be so far apart? Was it his fault that the woman beside him was now reduced to a shell of the strong woman he'd married? Where was the assertive, proud, and confident Rachel? What had happened to her?*

Slowly, his demeanor changed, and the answers to his questions crystallized into one thought: the only solution to the whole problem. Matt reached over, encircled Rachel with his arms, and pulled her towards him. Then he whispered something foreign to both of them, something he hadn't said in ages. "I love you."

The confession served as shock therapy, halting Rachel's tears. She looked up and searched his eyes for a hint of sincerity.

"I mean it." Matt said. "And we're going to make this thing work. If it means getting serious about having a baby, then I'll get serious."

"You're not kidding?" Rachel asked timidly.

"Not at all," Matt said confidently, "and if we can't have our own baby, we'll adopt."

Rachel straightened up, wiped her tear-stained face, and listened as Matt continued.

"In order for this plan to succeed, you must agree to two things: First, you must give up this obsession with the girl in Chicago."

Rachel fidgeted uncomfortably.

"Secondly, neither of us wants you taking any more drugs, certainly not while you're pregnant. So you must promise not to mention any dreams you might have. Understand? No more talk of the mystery girl. Nothing more about your dreams. Can you agree to that?"

"You mean, I don't have to take Haldol either?"

"As long as this approach works. OK?"

Baffled by his sudden change of heart, Rachel thought for a moment and then replied, "OK." She couldn't explain what was happening, but she wasn't about to contest it. She simply smiled and cuddled closer, relishing the warmth of Matt's embrace.

CHAPTER 5

Nobody's Child

A beam of sunlight ricocheted off the wooden slatted blinds and cut straight toward a row of photos displayed meticulously on top of an exquisite mahogany chest. The first photo depicted the birthing scene of a hollow-eyed, forty-something woman loosely cradling a newborn. The woman's limp, damp hair was matted behind her ears, and she appeared indifferent to the tiny bundle she held. The next picture was of a beautiful, auburn-haired preschool child performing with a miniature violin, followed by a 2 x 3-inch photo showing the same child several years older receiving an archery lesson from a tall, distinguished looking gentleman with a receding hairline. Among the larger 5 x 7-inch frames was a radiant, prepubescent girl dressed in a blue and silver soccer uniform proudly waving a trophy over her head.

Conspicuously absent from the group of photos were family scenes. Only one featured a man and woman together, each one having been pictured separately with the young girl. This photo showcased the older, handsomely dressed couple standing in a receiving line shaking hands with what appeared to be a Chinese delegation.

Above the chest, several elegantly framed awards complemented an adjacent trophy case filled with sports-related ribbons and trophies. Closer inspection revealed awards for archery, soccer, and swimming. Also arranged decoratively on the wall space above the chest were two diplomas—both doctoral degrees in cellular biology—one for the man and the other for the woman. As a whole, the study was tastefully decorated in English antiques, including the massive mahogany desk with its gold engraved nameplate: Dr. Forrest Prescott.

In the lavish foyer to the left of the study, the strident voices of a man and woman echoed off the sixteen-foot ceiling.

"I still can't believe you let that woman in yesterday," Forrest Prescott huffed. "Just what would've happened if I hadn't been here and called the police? You probably would've told her everything."

"Oh, please, give me a little more credit than that." A gaunt-faced, Catherine Prescott defended her actions. "You were caught off guard as well as I. Besides, I didn't want to appear rude. That would have played right into her suspicions."

"Well, you didn't have to encourage her either," Prescott snapped accusingly.

"I didn't. But it certainly would've helped if you had warned me."

"How could I have known some woman would come looking for our daughter? Chan was supposed to have sealed the records ages ago."

"That was the plan. And as far as I know, that still *is* the plan."

"Well, if this ever happens again, if anyone ever comes looking for Elise, say nothing and call security immediately. In the meantime, I'll see to it that we have no more surprise visits."

"Good. I prefer to eliminate surprises like that from my life."

"Don't worry, this woman, whoever she is, is messing with the wrong guy. I've already contacted James with instructions to trace her. She shouldn't be too hard to find."

"That reminds me, I found this photo in Elise's bureau this morning. She must've pulled it from the trash and taped it together." Catherine Prescott clutched a reconstructed photo of their unwelcome visitor. "Look, there's a name and address," she pointed out the writing on the back of the snapshot as she handed it to her husband.

Prescott mulled over the photo for a moment. "Hmmm . . . Rachel Duncan Hamilton, 1616 Oakwood Drive, Chapel Hill, North Carolina. Didn't notice the address before. Guess I won't need James' services after all. I'll just call Jeffrey instead. We'll handle this from a legal standpoint—trespassing and harassment. That ought to scare her off."

"But what if Elise tries to contact her?"

"If we have the address and Elise doesn't, how can she?"

"Are you suggesting I don't return the photo to her bureau? She'll know I've been snooping."

"Parental prerogative. She'll get over it."

"After her temper tantrum last night, I have no desire to get into another birth discussion with her. In fact, I refuse to." Catherine Prescott's torso stiffened.

"OK, OK. Put the photo back. It won't matter if she does try to contact this woman. After I establish the ground rules, there won't be any reciprocating on this—" he stopped to reread the name, "—this Rachel Hamilton's part. I guarantee that."

Forrest Prescott turned and disappeared into the study, leaving his wife standing alone in the front entranceway. "By the way," he called back, "what did you decide to do with Elise when you present your paper in Copenhagen?" Not waiting for her response, he situated himself behind his desk, picked up the telephone receiver, and began punching in numbers. Either he had already forgotten his question or else was not really interested in her response.

Catherine Prescott followed her husband into the study and didn't hesitate to interrupt him, "Since when did it become my responsibility to find child care?"

"She isn't a child anymore, or hadn't you noticed?"

"I'm perfectly aware of her developmental status. You know exactly what I mean. You agreed early on to handle those sort of things—it was part of our arrangement."

Prescott raised his head and spoke pointedly, "I'm sick and tired of your whining. You can't let a day go by without bringing that up. Our arrangement, if you remember, included you staying home to raise Elise until she started school. Now that's not what happened is it? So let's talk about keeping your end of the bargain first."

"You're such a chauvinist, such a self-centered prig. You pursue your research unfettered, but I'm expected to put everything I've worked for on hold."

"Don't forget, when Chan proposed this pregnancy, you're the one who agreed first, worried about your biological time clock running down."

"Ah, yes, and you needed a child so you could live vicariously through someone else's accomplishments. Trying to make up for your own failed childhood, I presume."

"Not even close. And since when did you become the resident analyst?" Prescott didn't wait for her response but purposely changed the subject. "I thought you were leaving to go to the lab. Don't let me keep you." He feigned concern only briefly, then shifted his attention to the phone once again and punched in the few remaining numbers.

"Don't worry about me," Catherine quipped sarcastically. Then she turned to leave the study, pausing long enough to offer a parting remark. "For your information, my Copenhagen trip is a go."

Prescott riveted to attention, catching her smirk as she rounded the corner and disappeared into the hallway.

"So, dear one," Catherine finished her remarks from the hallway, "you might want to spend a little time planning how you're going to handle the home front while I'm gone."

Seconds later the front door squeaked open, then slammed shut. Forrest rose from the desk, walked over to the window, and peered out from behind the blinds. He watched as his wife got into her Mercedes and drove down the long, winding drive—following her car until it was well out of sight. Then his eyes drank in the vast landscape that lay before him. He studied the meticulously trimmed shrubs, the manicured lawn, and the precisely positioned sculptures, smiling smugly as he mused, *this marriage has served me well.*

The next moment Prescott reflected on the unexpected visit from Rachel Hamilton. *I've worked too hard for all of this. It will be a cold day in hell before I let some woman—some crazed intruder—tamper with my success. No one is going to disrupt my domain. No one.*

CHAPTER 6

Clueless

Ring. *Ring. Ring.* Rachel grabbed
her purse, keys, and a bagel as she made her way to the back-
door, knowing if she stopped to answer the phone she would
be late to her appointment. But it was like the siren's voice
compelling her to answer, and she couldn't resist. She picked
up the receiver, "Hello?"

"Babe, I just got an emergency call—an attempted

75

suicide. I can't make the appointment. Sorry."

"Oh. . . ." she murmured. "Well, if I don't hurry, I won't make it either."

"So, I'll talk to you later?"

"Sure." Rachel answered curtly. There was a long pause.

"Are you OK?" Matt questioned.

"Yes. I better go though." Rachel said good-bye, sensing the loss again, the ongoing grief she felt each time she lost Matt to his medical world. A tinge of rage bubbled just beneath the surface. Rage she could never justify and therefore express. It was inevitable and expected to be second on his list of priorities. Medicine was his mistress—a respectable, culturally sanctioned mistress. It was useless to complain.

Rachel made her way to North Carolina Memorial Medical Center and found the doctor's office. The sign behind the receptionist read: "Judith MacKenzie, M.D. Maternal-Fetal Specialist." Rachel liked the idea of going to a woman obstetrician, and settling on Dr. MacKenzie, an adjunct professor at the med school, had been easy. Dr. MacKenzie specialized in problem pregnancies and maintained a private practice at Memorial, making her accessible to the community. Her reputation was excellent.

Rachel approached the receptionist and announced her arrival.

"Please take a seat, she'll be with you shortly."

Matt and Rachel were both pleased with their choice of an obstetrician, but coming alone for the initial interview wasn't part of the plan. Although Rachel knew she could handle it, she wished Matt had come. She wished she had expressed her disappointment when he called, and that for once, he had put her first—before the emergency, before some stranger. She needed his moral support, and sharing him with someone else, anyone else, was the last thing she wanted to do. Was it selfish to feel that way? Was it fair to expect her to have compassion for an unnamed, faceless patient when she was the one who needed him most?

Entering the "expecting mode" once again brought forth painful emotions. Fear of failure loomed before her, and she began questioning her own motivations. It was like Jenny had said on numerous occasions, "Why put yourself through the mental torture? Matt doesn't care." But Rachel knew she had to keep trying, even if she had to go it alone, even if she failed.

Although she eventually worked through the trauma of the first miscarriage, Matt never seemed to move beyond it. He essentially shut down whenever she brought up the subject of having a baby, and when she suggested returning to Chan for follow-up care, he exploded. Reading into Matt's overreaction, Rachel assumed Matt wrongly blamed Chan for losing the baby. She hoped he would eventually get past the blame, but when Chan received a huge grant to begin his own research institute, Matt celebrated his departure with unexpected fervor. Rachel never understood the relief Matt displayed the day Chan actually left the university, nor the distance that began to creep into their relationship.

While Rachel persisted in trying to carry a baby to term, Matt refused even to consider the idea. He allowed Rachel her obsession almost as an appeasement but never offered his support or demonstrated grief over subsequent pregnancy losses. Rachel attributed Matt's behavior to his demanding schedule. It didn't occur to her that there could be a deeper explanation or that her miscarriage had anything to do with the dreams that began shortly thereafter.

This time was different though. Matt seemed really serious about having a baby—about doing it right, and the appointment with MacKenzie was the first step in that direction. Rachel picked up a copy of *American Baby* as a distraction, hoping to calm her nerves and pass the time. She stopped momentarily at an article about preterm birth, then flipped through the pages, looking for another article of interest. "Sleep Loss: A Nightmare for Parents" caught her eye:

> New parents face an array of challenges and changes. It's as if passage into parenthood depends on fulfilling certain initiation rites—the first being how long one can last without sleep. This is closely followed by a test of one's ability to endure nightly awakenings every three hours, every night, for an undetermined period of time.
>
> Adapting to such a sudden change in sleep

patterns creates bodily chaos. It can also trans-
form the most patient, serene mother into a
crabby, irritable, bundle of nerves. But why does
sleep disruption alter disposition so drastically?
Sleep researchers offer some explanations. They
believe the amount of sleep an individual gets
isn't the only factor to consider; the sleep itself is
equally important.

There are two types of sleep: non-rapid eye
movement (NREM) and rapid eye movement
(REM). Dreams occur during REM sleep but
without both types of sleep, NREM and REM,
body rhythms are thrown out of balance. A closer
look at NREM sleep reveals four stages of sleep,
ranging from light sleep to deep sleep. Without
NREM sleep, one becomes physically tired.
Fatigue sets in. People routinely deprived of stage
four NREM sleep become apathetic and
depressed.

Just as NREM sleep renews us physically,
REM sleep refreshes us mentally. An insufficient
supply of REM sleep produces anxious, irritable
people who have trouble with social interactions.

The majority of REM sleep occurs in the
early morning hours, becoming more predominant
as daylight approaches. It is also the time most
dreams occur. The first period of REM sleep lasts

only 15 minutes, but by morning, the periods become longer and the dreams more bizarre. . . .

"Ms. Hamilton?" A nurse holding a folder looked around the waiting room for a responsive face.

"That would be me," Rachel answered.

"Please follow me." They made their way down the hall, stopping beside an open doorway. "The doctor will talk with you in here," the nurse pointed into a tastefully decorated office. "Please have a seat."

Masking her anxiety, Rachel mentally told herself not to ramble or fidget. She straightened her jean skirt and tried to get comfortable in one of the wing chairs positioned in front of the desk. Diplomas of every size and shape decorated the wall before her. *Bachelor of Science in Biology from Notre Dame. Long way to go for school . . . unless of course you're from Indiana. . . .*

"Rachel? So glad to meet you." A strawberry-blonde with freckles sprinkled across her nose breezed into the room. Her long, wavy hair was tied back loosely with a covered rubber band, and her lab coat was a bit oversized. Rachel could tell she wasn't concerned about being a fashion statement. Holding out her hand, Dr. MacKenzie smiled warmly. "I feel like I know you already. Matt always spoke fondly of you."

"Oh. . . ." Rachel stammered, taken aback by Dr. MacKenzie's charm and especially by her reference to Matt. "I didn't realize Matt knew you."

"Well, our paths don't cross regularly now, but when we were in residency, we ran into each other quite a bit. I remember you two were married then. In fact, everyone knew Matt was 'taken.'"

Rachel felt a twinge of jealousy seeping in and wasn't sure she liked the idea of Matt having any kind of relationship with such a magnetic woman. "You probably saw more of him than I did back then." Rachel tried to sound unaffected by the comment.

"Oh, I don't know. I didn't really see much of anyone during residency. I was doing well to keep my head above water. Survival was the name of the game."

Rachel didn't have time to respond as Dr. MacKenzie jumped right into the interview.

"So, how can I help you? The form you filled out says you've had a problem with miscarriages."

"The only pregnancy I carried for any length of time was the first one."

"And how long was that?"

"About five months."

"So you were at least 20 weeks along?"

"Yes, the baby was kicking pretty hard by then."

"Were the other miscarriages second trimester?"

"No, usually early on. Six to eight weeks."

"Can you tell me a little about the second trimester miscarriage? Did anything specific precipitate it?"

"I don't remember much. Just that it was an awful

experience—rather fuzzy. Dr. Chan handled everything. It's probably in my chart somewhere."

"Dr. Robert Chan?" A bewildered look accompanied the question.

"Yes. Matt was working for him at the time."

"I never knew he did regular obstetrics."

"I think taking me on was a favor to Matt."

"Ah ... that's strange...." Dr. MacKenzie shook her head, obviously having a difficult time processing the information.

"What do you mean, 'strange'?"

"It's just that when I was in residency, Chan had a reputation of being outside the mainstream. Politically active, pushing for things nobody wanted. He didn't seem concerned with normal births."

"What are you talking about?"

"For one thing, he wanted to force every obstetrical training program to include an abortion rotation. It didn't fit with what we were doing—bringing life into the world. No one felt comfortable with his ideas."

"So what happened?"

"Oh, I don't know. We moved on. I didn't hear much about him after a while. I just never understood how he could be doing research on in vitro fertilization and at the same time pushing for more abortions. It didn't make sense."

"Are you saying he wasn't competent or something?"

"No, no. I'm sure he's quite competent. I personally had

a problem with the man. It has nothing to do with you. And really I shouldn't be talking about it." Dr. MacKenzie quickly changed the subject. "I'll try to get your records. That'll tell me about the past. But let's talk about now. Are you currently taking any drugs?"

"Not any more."

"What do you mean?"

"Matt quit prescribing sleeping pills when he got serious about having a baby. He wanted to give me Haldol, but then things changed—"

"Haldol? He wanted you on an antipsychotic? What in heaven's name for?"

"Oh, it's a long story. Do you think the sleeping pills had something to do with my miscarriages?"

"Depends. Some medications are definitely off limits during pregnancy. We'll check on that." She made a note and then continued. "Do you mind telling me why he prescribed sleeping pills?"

"My dreams."

"Dreams?"

"Nightmares, really. Matt didn't like to see me upset."

"So he put you on barbituates?" MacKenzie's astonishment mounted.

"On and off, when the dreams got bad."

"I know they suppress REM sleep, but what a hassle. Why didn't he just try dream analysis?"

"I guess this way was easier for him."

"Gee," MacKenzie laughed, "what good is a psychiatrist husband if you can't get free therapy?"

"Trust me, I get plenty of that." They both laughed. Rachel sensed a camaraderie with this woman and knew she was going to like her.

MacKenzie grew serious again. "Let's move on. Do you smoke?"

"No."

"Are you routinely exposed to environmental hazards—X-rays, chemicals?"

"Don't think so."

"Is there a history of pregnancy loss in your family?"

"No, not that I'm aware of."

"Anyone ever tell you that you have a T-shaped uterus or incompetent cervix?"

"No."

"Do you know your blood type?"

"I think it's AB."

"How about Matt's?"

"I'm not sure, but I know they gave me a shot of Rhogam after the first miscarriage. I'm RH negative. Do you think that's the reason I'm miscarrying so much?"

"Could be. Sometimes blood incompatibility between mother and baby plays a role. If the baby's type is different, your body may treat it like a foreign object and develop antibodies against it. We'll check it out." She jotted another note down and then resumed her questioning. "Do you remember if you had the flu or a viral infection during the time of any of your pregnancies?"

"No."

"Were you ever checked for an ongoing infection in your uterus?"

"No."

"One last question. Have you ever had an abortion?"

"No." Rachel had a pained expression on her face.

"I'm sorry—it's a sensitive question for a lot of women—but I have to ask. Studies show a three to nine fold increase in miscarriages in women who've had abortions." Dr. MacKenzie closed the chart she had been writing notes in, folded her hands, and sat back in her chair. "We definitely have some areas to explore."

Rachel looked up expectantly. "Then you think I'll be able to have a baby?"

"Possibly. Let's hope so."

They never got their tree until the week of Christmas, and since Rachel insisted on a real tree, Matt always carved out time in his busy schedule to cut one down. This year, Skip—Jenny's husband—accompanied Matt on his mission to the outskirts of town. The ritual involved tromping through the woods until they found just the right tree. Rachel promised a reward of hot, spiced tea upon their return, then she and Jenny settled into their favorite chairs in front of the fire to sample the tea and catch up on the latest news.

"I don't know how you can trust Matt to pick out a good tree." Jenny paused to blow steam off her tea. "I always have to supervise Skip's choices."

"You'd be surprised. Matt has a much better sense of size than I do. I can never tell if it'll be too tall or too short. Besides, it's easier to let Matt pick it out, then there's no argument."

"You've got a point there. . . . Hey, have you noticed Matt and Skip spending more time together? Seems chopping wood fits them both, therapeutic or something."

"I think it's a guy thing. Matt has to fill his spare time with something, or he'll go crazy. At least chopping wood is productive."

"Don't you think it's not so much a guy thing as a doctor thing?" Jenny looked pensive, almost analytical. Skip was a radiologist, and Jenny and Rachel often discussed the parallels between their doctor-husbands.

"Maybe fits with the type A personality . . . push, push, push. Although I've noticed a change in Matt lately. He's less driven."

"Really? That classifies as a miracle in my book. Dr. Matthew Hamilton, slowing down. Hard to believe. Could this really be happening?"

"Hold on. I didn't say he'd completely changed. I said, I've noticed a change. It's too early to tell." Rachel hesitated.

"But maybe, just maybe, it is the beginning of a new direction. I mean, ever since he decided to have a baby, it's like he has a new perspective or something."

"Like what?"

"Well, for instance, you know how he never wants to go with me to the Christmas Eve service? How I always have to go alone?"

"Oh yeah. . . ."

"Well, this year, for some unknown reason, he's agreed to go. No grumbling or anything."

"Sounds serious . . . seriously wonderful!"

Rachel didn't share Jenny's optimism; she'd been disappointed too many times before. Her thoughts shifted. "Have you gotten Skip's Christmas present yet?"

"Just yesterday. Got him a new watch."

"You have it so easy. I'd never find a watch good enough for Matt. He'd want a 'state of the art' one with a GPS or something, and that's definitely out of my league." Rachel rolled her eyes.

"A what?"

"A global positioning system." Rachel caught Jenny's puzzled expression and added, "Don't even ask." They both laughed.

"So what are you going to get him?"

"Probably something practical. I saw a pressure cooker in that little kitchen store in the mall. Some super, deluxe model imported from Spain—a Fagor."

"A pressure cooker?"

"I blew his up. Remember?"

"How could I forget? You're dangerous, Rachel. That's all there is to it." Jenny chuckled.

"Hey, it's not my fault Matt wasn't here when I tried to use it. And besides, at least I was fixing dinner—that should count for something."

Jenny shook her head, "You two are such an unlikely pair. How in the world did you ever get together?"

"Believe me, I've asked myself that question a million times. All I can say is, it was meant to be. . . ."

CHAPTER 7

China Syndrome

The morning was still young when Rachel sat down in front of her computer conveniently located in a built-in space adjacent to the kitchen. She was on her second cup of decaf and had just checked her E-mail when the idea hit her. *Maybe I can find Elise Prescott on the Internet.*

Impulsively, Rachel pulled up the Yahoo search screen

on her computer and typed in Elise's name under the "411 people" E-mail category. Before she could blink, an E-mail address for an Elise Prescott appeared on the screen: striker001@aol.com. She checked to see if the name matched a Downers Grove address. *Yes! It all fits. It has to be Elise!* Barely containing her excitement, Rachel looked to see if Elise was on-line. She clicked "locate member" and waited. Finally a small screen popped up informing her, that striker001 was not currently signed on. *Elise is probably in school this time of day anyway. This time of day!* Rachel quickly looked at the clock and realized she'd been sitting way too long in front of the computer. *Rats. Gotta get to my appointment with MacKenzie!* She carefully added Elise's name to her Buddy list and resolved to look for her again that evening. . . . *I bet I can find her in a soccer chat room. . . .*

A tall, lanky, college kid wearing a flannel shirt and a faded Carolina baseball cap shuffled nervously in line. Matt waited patiently behind him, even though the errand was taking much longer than anticipated. *Why didn't I order them by phone? But I have to do this in person. I can't take any chances.*

Matt's standard operating procedure was to avoid ordering things over the phone—even Chinese take-out. It was an irrational aversion, a quirk Rachel had pointed out on more than one occasion. He couldn't explain its origin, much less his compulsion to hang on to it, so they both just accepted the custom as they did his other idiosyncrasies. Matt realized that standing in line at the florist shop was totally unnecessary, yet he was there nonetheless. He smiled to himself, knowing Rachel's explanation. "Face it. It's a control thing. You're such a perfectionist, and you want to make sure everyone else is, too."

Rachel thought Matt was transparent, seeing straight to his heart, reading the writing etched in stone. She never hesitated to offer her psychoanalysis of his actions. "Somehow, your mother's death produced this fear of losing, of not being in control. Somehow you think you're responsible for her death, and you think attaining perfection will keep tragedy at arm's length. The real problem is, you don't trust God and you think that by being God you can keep things like that from ever happening again. But you're wrong." Then she'd kiss him and remind him, "One day you'll have to face your fears."

The college kid ordered the same as everyone else. When Matt stepped forward, the clerk looked up mechanically. "Roses?"

"No." Matt responded flatly. He didn't offer an alternative fast enough, so the clerk began swirling his hand above his head as if to pull a response out of the air.

"Have another suggestion?"

"Daisies." Matt replied tentatively.

Interpreting Matt's carefully calculated response as indecision, the man offered his expertise. "Well, no one sends daisies on Valentine's Day."

"Says who?"

"Hey, Mister, you can send whatever you like. I'm just here to sell flowers."

"Well then, that's what I want."

"Fine. Did you want a delivery card with it?"

"Ah . . . no, I'll just pick out one of these and take it with me." Matt gestured toward a rack of cards to his right.

"Who do you want them delivered to?"

"Rachel Hamilton, 1616 Oakwood Drive."

"No problem. Send 'em right out."

Matt paid for the card and flowers and jumped into his car. He wanted to surprise Rachel by meeting her before her doctor's appointment. Driving down the road, his thoughts rambled.

Ever since the night Matt made the deal with Rachel to have a baby—which included her promise to avoid mentioning her dreams or the fantasy girl in Chicago—their relationship had taken an upward turn. It felt like they were back in med school, before the miscarriage, before they had started growing apart and Rachel had become delusional about having a daughter. He was glad to move forward, glad to leave those nightmare days behind.

Matt's timing was perfect. He watched as Rachel breezed up the sidewalk and through the revolving doors into the hospital's main lobby. Her single-minded focus—making it to the elevator before the doors closed—made her oblivious to employees and visitors meandering through the lobby. Besides, med students and residents rarely used the front entrance, so the possibility of running into Matt was the farthest thing from her mind. He was supposed to be making rounds with his students that very moment. It was not surprising that she failed to notice Matt's presence as he unobtrusively fell in step behind her.

Rachel sprinted the last couple of yards, crossing the finish line just as the elevator door closed and right before Matt leaped aboard behind her.

"Got ya!" he teased, wrapping his arms around her waist and pulling her towards him.

Startled, Rachel twisted around to face him. "Oh! Darling, don't scare me like that."

"Couldn't help myself. You were such an easy target."

"Glad I could provide entertainment."

"Me, too." He leaned forward and kissed her tenderly on the forehead. Then he released his embrace and stepped back while he fished for the card from his pocket. "I wanted to catch you before you got to MacKenzie's office," he explained. "I have a little proposition for you." He whipped out the card and presented it with a bow, "Will you be my valentine?"

Not missing a beat, Rachel flashed a smile and sashayed closer. She stood on her tiptoes and put both arms around his neck. "Only if you promise to be mine." Then she pulled his mouth down to hers, discarding any sense of propriety.

They were still glued together when the elevator doors suddenly opened, providing an unobstructed view for a waiting group of residents whose spontaneous applause terminated the impromptu rendezvous. Matt ignored the audience as he stepped out of the elevator alongside Rachel.

"Thanks for the ride . . . and my card." Rachel smiled, holding the card over her heart.

"My pleasure." Matt winked, then hopped back on the elevator to catch a ride back down. Rachel blew him a kiss, spun around, and hurried off to her appointment.

The waiting room was full of expectant mothers in varying stages of pregnancy. Rachel scanned the room for a vacant seat next to a nonpregnant woman. Her plan was to avoid, if at all possible, having to chat and compare pregnancy notes. It was just too painful, and besides, her own experience was limited at best, and she had nothing to contribute to such a conversation. If she were really honest with herself, however, Rachel would admit that she actually resented those rounded, glowing, "women with child" types, and she just didn't trust her cynical side not to surface.

The seat next to an attractive, young, Asian woman was the obvious choice. The woman, preoccupied with reading a letter, appeared to be a safe bet even though Rachel couldn't be sure. The woman didn't look pregnant, but then, neither did Rachel. Although officially pregnant for ten full weeks,

Rachel didn't think she qualified as a real pregnant woman. It was still too early to predict, and she didn't dare consider her fate. MacKenzie was right; she must limit her focus: "One day at a time." That was all she could handle anyway.

Rachel settled down just as a nurse came out and announced, "Dr. MacKenzie has been involved with a difficult delivery this morning and will be late getting here. Anyone who'd like to reschedule may speak with the receptionist."

"Hurry up and wait . . . the story of my life," Rachel muttered under her breath, prompting the Asian woman to glance up briefly. Rachel noted the woman's meticulously tailored suit and neatly coiffured hairdo and wondered if she was a journalist or lawyer. *If not,* Rachel thought, *she could certainly play the part on TV.* Rachel decided to take a chance and turned sideways in her seat, clearing her throat before initiating a conversation. "Looks like we're stuck here for a while."

The woman again looked up from her letter, this time cutting her tear-filled, green eyes directly into Rachel's. Immediately Rachel realized she had intruded and quickly offered an apology. "I'm sorry; I didn't mean to bother you."

"Oh, that's alright. It's . . . it's nothing." The woman folded the letter and slipped it into her briefcase. "I shouldn't let it upset me. There's nothing I can do anyway." She heaved a sigh. "Just wasted energy . . . it's a mess. An awful mess."

Rachel sat quietly and nodded.

"My cousin lives in China. She's pregnant."

"That's a mess?"

"Over there it is. It's her third pregnancy, and the government is pressuring her to abort."

"She has two children already?"

"No. They only allow one per family, and she had an abortion the last time. She can't bear to do it again. She's frantic. I don't know what she's going to do. She's put it off for as long as she can, and any day now they're going to come get her, take her to a clinic, and force her to abort. I know exactly what's going to happen, and I can't do anything about it." The woman shook her head in obvious distress.

"I'm so sorry."

"The irony is, she can get pregnant. I can't. I'm the one that should be living over there, not her." The woman stopped abruptly and looked apologetically at Rachel. "Forgive me. I shouldn't be dumping this on you. I don't even know you."

"Hey, it's alright. I don't mind. And as far as not knowing me, we can remedy that." Rachel smiled compassionately and extended her hand, "Hi, I'm Rachel."

The woman responded in kind, "Hi, I'm Helen."

Rachel donned a serious expression, "I take it you're not pregnant."

"Good guess. But it's not because I haven't tried."

"Been trying a long time?"

"Seems like forever. I've tried everything—even been ripped off by a few I.V.F. clinics."

"I.V.F.?"

"In vitro fertilization. They're more than happy to take your money but then can't promise you anything. I'm convinced most of them are scams. When I found out about their high failure rates, I knew we'd been taken."

"So, why do you think MacKenzie can help you?"

"Oh, I'm not here for that. I came to interview MacKenzie for an article I'm researching. I suppose I *could* ask her about my situation . . . maybe . . . but short of immaculate conception, I doubt she can help me."

"She might be able to. She has lots of success stories. Approaches everything from a common-sense angle—eat right, eliminate pollutants and toxins from your environment. Things like that. For me, conceiving isn't a problem, just carrying to term; she has me using relaxation techniques—thinks stress is my biggest problem."

"Well, my biggest problem is divine retribution, and you can't fight that."

"Are you saying God is responsible for your infertility?"

"No. I blame myself. I just think I'm getting what I deserve."

"So you think God's punishing you?"

"Maybe not directly, but when you fool around like I did in college, what do you expect?"

Rachel was silent.

"I slept around, got an infection, and scarred my fallopian tubes. Like I said, what do you expect?"

"I understand about 'reaping what you sow,' but that's different from saying God's punishing you."

"Maybe so, but I can't explain it any other way. Is my cousin 'reaping what she's sown'? Does she deserve what's happening to her?"

"I'm not suggesting she deserves anything. But you can't make God responsible for the evil men do."

"Why not? Isn't he in charge?"

"Of course, but he doesn't make people sin. They do that just fine on their own—without any help from God or anybody else."

"Well, that's true. I suppose there's plenty of evil to go around. Look at my cousin's situation: forced abortion is a way of life. There's no pretense of compassion at all. The Chinese government even provides mobile abortion units. Drive-by abortions—how morally depraved can you get? Take a look at this." Helen opened her briefcase and pulled out a colorful leaflet. The photo on the front cover flaunted a doctor standing inside a fully equipped mobile medical suite.

Rachel took the leaflet and studied it momentarily. The doctor's entreating smile and the bucket at the foot of a gurney imparted chilling insight, and suddenly Rachel felt nauseated. Something deep inside stirred a vague sense of recognition, generating an uneasy feeling. It was an irrational response, she knew, yet she couldn't quite shake it. Posing a question to Helen finally redirected her thoughts. "How do you know they do abortions in there? Can you read Chinese?"

"A little. My mom taught me some, and I picked up some when I spent a summer with my cousin."

"So what does this say?"

"Oh . . . it's an abortion unit all right. 'A convenient way to comply with government regulation.' Funny thing . . . it's funded by an American Company."

"What?"

"Right here, it says Biotechnologies Research International, USA. Ever heard of it?"

"I'm not sure. It sounds—"

The nurse reappeared at the door. "Mrs. Bohannon, Dr. MacKenzie can see you now."

"That's me." Helen stood up, briefcase in hand. "Thanks for listening. I can get pretty carried away."

"Not a problem." Rachel watched Helen follow the nurse out of the waiting room.

CHAPTER 8

Cyberspace

R achel lugged in the groceries, bag
by bag. According to Dr. MacKenzie, it was important to
eliminate all possible stressors, including heavy-laden grocery
bags. So why was she even getting the groceries at all? It was
a logistical matter: there was nothing to eat; they were out of
milk, and Matt was not available—as usual.

Rachel put away the frozen items first, then checked the

answering machine for messages. She pressed the play button and a computer-generated voice announced: You have one message. Then Matt's voice came across loud and clear. "Hey Babe, don't wait dinner on me. Looks like it's gonna be awhile before I can break away."

Rachel glanced at the clock—6:00 P.M. *Don't worry about me. I have a little unfinished business.* She pulled out a newly purchased container of hummus, opened it, tore off a few pieces of pita bread, then piled it all onto a plate and made her way over to her computer. Carefully seating herself with makeshift dinner in hand, Rachel went straight into her buddy list and clicked on Elise's screen name: striker001. But before she hit locate, Rachel stopped herself, taking a moment to replay Jenny's chastisement in her mind: "You're going overboard with this thing. You have no business searching for this girl. Think about what you're doing. It's not rational."

Rachel didn't dwell on the scolding. She chose instead to dismiss Jenny's psychological assessment and proceed with her search. *So I'm crazy. I can live with it.* She hit *locate* and waited. All of a sudden, a pop-up screen gave her the response she'd been anticipating. *Yes! Success!* Rachel stood up in excitement, accidentally knocking her plate of food on the floor. She ignored the mess, totally preoccupied with her victory. After numerous failed attempts, *finally* she had timed it right, *finally* Elise was on-line.

Rachel wasted no time entering the soccer chat room. Her intention was to "lurk," to sit unnoticed and silently follow the unfolding conversation between the soccer players on-line, including Elise Prescott.

Girlkicker:	Going to soccer camp this year?
Striker001:	Of course, my whole team's going.
Girlkicker:	Where?
Striker001:	UNC.
Girlkicker:	No way!
Striker001:	Yes way! It's an awesome place. My team went last year, and there were girls from everywhere—even Sweden.
Girlkicker:	Sweden?
Eurosport:	Yes! UNC rules! All the best women's soccer players go there. They've won at least fourteen national titles.
Goaliegirl:	That's where I want to go to college, but it's hard to get in out-of-state.
Striker001:	That's what I'm told. Does it count if you were born in NC? It's not my fault my parents moved to Chicago when I was still a baby.
Girlkicker:	Doesn't count.
Striker001:	Guess I'll have to move there then.
Goaliegirl:	You and every other soccer player in the country.
Girlkicker:	Hey, Eurosport! Haven't heard from you in a long time. What gives?
Eurosport:	Lots of homework. How was your season?

P r o g e n y

Girlkicker: Lost in the state finals to the number-one ranked team.

Eurosport: So sorry. Had any college offers?

Girlkicker: UNC and U. Conn.

Striker001:   How did you get Carolina to look at you?

Girlkicker: Playing in tournaments and being on the olympic development team helped.

Striker001:   Don't they recruit from soccer camp, too?

Girlkicker: Sometimes, but I couldn't afford to go to camp.

Striker001:   I hope they notice me at camp. It would help my chances of getting into UNC, wouldn't it?

Eurosport: Anything would help. You need all the chances you can get if you're serious about going to UNC.

Striker001:   I'll tell my father that's why I have to go to camp.

Eurosport: Is he still giving you a hard time about going back there?

Striker001:   Yeah, he's got a hang-up about me being so far away from home. Thinks I need special protection.

Eurosport: Weird.

Striker001:   I'll say! He says someone might kidnap me or something.

Girlkicker: Double weird.

Eurosport: I don't understand. Why did he let you go last year and not now?

Striker001:   Not sure. But he has to let me go. My coach is

	requiring the whole team to go. If he doesn't let me go, I'll run away. I swear I will.
Eurosport:	Bad idea. Who would pay for camp?
Striker001:	I don't know but I don't need their money . . . . I can fend for myself.
Goaliegirl:	Good luck with that.
Eurosport:	Hey, I'll take their money. I need a car.
Striker001:	You're already driving? When did you turn 16?
Girlkicker:	I haven't, but I have my learner's permit. I'm planning ahead.
Striker001:	I won't get my permit 'til next summer.
Eurosport:	Bummer! So what kind of cool car are your parents gonna buy you?
Striker001:	I don't know, and I don't care.

Rachel's mind drifted away from the chat room as she debated sending Elise a message on-line. There were so many unanswered questions: Why did she feel connected to Elise? And was it significant that she was born in North Carolina? Although her immediate impulse was to reach out to the girl, she hesitated. What would it accomplish? If anything, an impromptu contact would probably do little more than frighten her. Besides, if Elise told her parents about Rachel's Internet contact, pandemonium could break loose. Matt would go ballistic. Fighting her impulse was definitely the best course of action at this point.

Regardless, Rachel couldn't help playing a hypothetical message over in her mind: "Hi, I think we're related. I sense a mystical bond between us. I know none of it makes sense, and I can't explain why I feel this way, but trust me . . . even though my husband thinks I'm psycho. By the way, your parents don't take kindly to me either."

Maybe I can just pretend I'm another soccer girl who happens to live in Chapel Hill? That would establish common ground . . . but then what?

With limited knowledge of soccer, it wouldn't take long for Elise to figure out Rachel didn't belong in a soccer chat room at all. Of course, she could always research the game and then chat, but that would take time, and she wanted to interrogate Elise now! Again, she held back her impulse, knowing that in order to connect meaningfully and to prevent a major war with Matt, she needed a better approach.

Then it occurred to her: *Look up Elise's birth certificate— that's how I can find out exactly where she was born.* But how could she get a copy? From experience as a journalism student trying to do research, Rachel knew it would take an act of God to obtain a birth certificate from the North Carolina Bureau of Vital Records and Statistics. They refused to give out copies to anyone except family or those with special written permission. And the probability of the Prescotts giving her written permission was zero. That was a fact. But no one could stop her from trying.

Still, Rachel knew the futility of such an escapade. She had once traipsed all the way down to Orange County to complete a journalism assignment only to be denied access to birth certificate records by a receptionist who relished control over the situation and who wasn't the least bit interested in bending the rules for Rachel. That incident seemed so distant now, so far removed from her life. The miscarriage had changed everything—demanding every last ounce of strength within her to push through her remaining coursework. Paralyzed by the emotional trauma, Rachel had watched as her career plans dissolved right before her eyes. And when the nightmares began, her coping mechanisms failed entirely.

Each day when twilight approached, panic struck. Haunted by the thought that she would again be transported into a world where she'd be forced to save an unknown child, Rachel became frantic. In her dreams, the scenario was always the same: the bad guys hunted her down, and she was always running—the outcome never resolved.

It was inevitable that she became obsessed with avoiding her dreams, and so Matt finally decided "enough was enough" and began prescribing sleeping pills. Conveniently, one of the side effects of the drugs was to suppress REM sleep, and so the dreams disappeared altogether. This pleased them both. But Matt ignored the drug-related repercussions for Rachel, considering it a small price to pay for peace of mind. It was a sacrifice they both endured.

Now that she was no longer taking the drugs, Rachel was

slowly reclaiming her life. She delighted in her restored self—the transformation as welcome as it was vital. Strangely though, the dreams—which Jenny kept saying were a result of her unconscious desire to nurture and protect—had been replaced with an obsession to rescue Elise. It was as if she were acting out a play in which Rachel was the protagonist and Elise was the victim. It wasn't rational, but then, neither were her dreams.

Helen jumped up to greet MacKenzie as she emerged from the obstetrical suite. It was late evening, and MacKenzie looked exhausted as she dragged herself out the front doors. Helen met MacKenzie's eyes with an intense expression.

"I'm sorry I couldn't spend more time with you earlier today. I had a late start and lots of patients to see. Thanks for meeting me."

"I know you're busy, but I need to talk with you—a few unanswered questions."

"Not a problem. You can walk me to my car and ask me all the questions you want."

"Excellent. You know the article I was writing a while ago about how in vitro fertilization might affect the offspring?"

"Yes, I remember."

"Well, all the research on reproductive technologies brought me straight back to Dr. Robert Chan."

"I'm not surprised. He's widely published. Remember

what I told you about him, from my days as a resident?"

"I know, I know. That's one reason I'm back—trying to understand something. If he ended up doing abortions like you said, why would he be interested in infertility?"

"It's a mystery to me."

"Do you know any specifics about his research now?"

"All I know is that he's got a huge setup over in Research Triangle Park—Biotechnologies Research International."

"What?" Helen's mouth dropped open, and her eyes widened.

"Biotec—"

"I heard, I heard." Helen blurted out, her shocked look still lingering.

"What's the problem?"

Helen detached herself momentarily and mumbled, "Nothing I can do, nothing you can do. . . ."

"Certainly not if you don't tell me what the problem is."

Helen regained her composure. "It concerns my cousin—a leaflet she sent me from China. I just didn't put it together until now."

"Put what together?"

Helen didn't reply, as her dejection quickly turned to anger. "If Chan is involved in this. . . . "

"You'll do what? Please quit talking in circles."

"I apologize." Helen made a point of stifling her emotions. "It's a personal thing. I didn't mean to get off on it. Can we just drop it?"

"It's your call."

"Good—I really need your input on a few things. To begin with, do you know anything about a Dr. Forrest Prescott?"

"Prescott? Never heard of him. Is he a reproductive endocrinologist?"

"No, a molecular biologist. I've asked around, but no one seems to know much about him. I even called his home in Chicago and tried to set up an interview."

"No luck?"

"None whatsoever. They weren't very accommodating."

"Well, I can't help you either. Can't place him at all."

"That's all right; I'll figure it out. The other thing I need from you is more info about the technologies we discussed. Do you have time for dinner? I need to verify a few things."

"Not tonight. It's my night at the teen clinic. I volunteer my services—" she checked her watch "—and I was supposed to be there by now. I can't believe it's so late!"

"I'm sorry; I didn't mean to hold you up."

"You're not." MacKenzie smiled reassuringly "I haven't even gotten to my car yet." She waved towards a car on the other side of the sparsely filled parking lot.

"Well, this certainly was poor timing on my part." Helen sighed.

"Couldn't be helped."

The wind picked up, and MacKenzie tightened her coat

more securely around her waist as she led the way, weaving around the few vehicles in their path. After a moment of deep thought, Helen shifted the tone of the conversation, shaking her head in dismay. "I still can't get over the story you told me about that couple who hired a surrogate mother to carry a child to term for them and then sued her because she wanted to have an abortion."

"That's nothing," MacKenzie perked up. "Did you read about the custody battle over the frozen embryos?"

"No, but a lawyer friend told me about it. Seems all these new technologies are throwing the legal world into a frenzy. They can't keep up with it all." Helen drew in a cold breath and continued. "The one that takes the cake, though, is that bizarre case where a child was conceived by donor sperm and egg and then the couple divorced and the judge ruled that the 'father' didn't have to pay child support because he wasn't the biological father!"

"Actually," MacKenzie broke in, "the court ruled that the child was 'nobody's child' since there was no genetic link to either one of the couple."

"It's crazy."

"I'll say. But then, we live in a crazy world." MacKenzie threw back her head and laughed. By now, they had crossed the parking lot and reached her car. She apologized as she opened the door. "I wish I had more time to talk."

"Me, too. We'll just have to do this another time. I'll call first."

"Great. See you later." MacKenzie got into her little Volkswagon convertible, started up the engine, then pulled out of her parking space, leaving Helen standing alone in the middle of the doctors' parking lot. Helen's gaze followed the headlights as they disappeared around a bend. Suddenly, she felt the cold night air breathe down her neck and a piercing chill sliced straight through her jacket. She hadn't noticed the dark before, but now it was unavoidable. The night seemed to envelop everything and would have except for a few, isolated streetlights. The silhouettes of barren tree limbs reached out to her like spindly fingers, spurring her onward.

She quickly retraced her steps up the hill towards the general parking lot. Normally, the hike back to her car would not have concerned her. But tonight, for some odd reason, she didn't feel safe. Although there was no one in sight, she had the sense that someone was watching her—from a distance. She surveyed the area before her, then scanned both sides of the lot. Nothing. No sounds. No movement. *It must be my imagination.*

Finally reaching her car, Helen fumbled for her keys and exhaled a sigh of relief as she inserted the key into the lock. *That's funny. How could it be unlocked? I'm sure I locked it.* Cautiously opening the door, she immediately realized someone had rifled through her things; her papers and folders were in disarray, and the glove compartment was wide open. *Why would someone be in my car? Why would they care about my notes?*

CHAPTER 9

Runaway

"I said she's gone!" Catherine Prescott yelled back down the stairwell to her husband.

"That's not possible. I had the alarm set. She couldn't have gotten out of this house without setting it off."

"I guess she foiled you," Catherine scoffed, still clad in her robe and slippers. "Her bedroom window's wide open . . . must've climbed through and jumped."

"From the second story?"

"No other explanation."

"When's the last time you saw her?" Forrest Prescott huffed as he made his way back up the spiral staircase.

"Last night at dinner—after the blowup over her genetics homework assignment."

"You mean you didn't see her after that?" He followed Catherine down the hallway to Elise's room.

"No, I just assumed she was on her computer—like always."

"Well, this isn't like always. You know what her counselor said might happen if she—"

"Was agitated? Became despondent?"

"Enough already!" Forrest cut his wife off as he entered Elise's room. "I handled her the best way I could. I'd already given in to her demands to go to soccer camp—and that against all rational judgment."

Forrest paused to survey Elise's room, "Her bed hasn't been slept in."

"Obviously. Doesn't take a rocket scientist to figure that one out."

Forrest ignored his wife's sarcasm. "Anything missing?"

"Just a small overnight bag and Rachel Hamilton's photo."

"Great." He shook his head in frustration. "That's all we need—Elise to make contact with that woman. I suppose I'll have to contact the others about the possibility."

"You mean Chan?"

"Chan's the least of my worries. The other guys are a lot less tolerant."

"She can't have gotten very far."

"We hope." Forrest's tone lacked any hint of encouragement. "Get on the phone and call the sheriff."

They made their way back downstairs, and Catherine headed towards the kitchen. "I'll make my call from in here."

"Fine. I'll be in the study. Be sure you tell them she's a juvenile, and don't forget to tell them about her counselor's warning while you're at it."

"Why would I tell them that our daughter might be suicidal? How will that look?"

"I don't care how it looks. Do it. Tell them she could be violent to herself or others. We need to get them moving on this!"

Catherine entered the kitchen, poured herself a cup of coffee, and was about to pick up the wall phone when Forrest shouted to her from his study. "Catherine, get in here, now!"

"What's the problem?" Catherine called back, making an about-face and joining him in the study. Immediately she saw the open metal file box on his desk. "So, what have we here? Looks like someone's rummaged through your important papers."

Forrest leaned heavily against the back of the leather chair and sighed.

"What do you think she was looking for? Can you tell if she took anything?"

"I'll have to take an inventory, but it doesn't look like anything's gone. I think she was just looking for money. She took the cash I had stashed in this cigar humidor." He held up an empty container and heaved another disgruntled sigh. "There wasn't much in there, so I doubt—"

"Rap, rap, rap." The brass front door knocker clanked loudly.

"Who in the world would be here this early in the morning?" Catherine barely peered out of the window before a shocked look spread over her face. "It's a state trooper. Looks like Charlie Wilcox. You better get it."

Forrest hurried out of his study into the foyer. Within seconds, he pulled open the massive mahogany door. "Hello Charlie, what can I do for you?"

"Missing a daughter?" He pointed toward his cruiser where Elise was slumped down in the backseat—her head bowed, her shoulders sagging.

"Well . . . ah . . . yes." Prescott stuttered. "I'm totally baffled by this."

"I picked her up off the turnpike—thumbing for a ride. When I realized it was *your* daughter, I decided to bring her straight home. Do you have any idea why she would be out like that?"

"No." Catherine Prescott appeared around the door, curtly responding to the officer's question. "We just discovered she was missing. I was getting ready to call the sheriff's office."

"Glad I could save you the trouble."

"Did you say she was hitchhiking?" Catherine was fully engaged in the conversation by now.

"Yep. We've been watching for runaways. Seems to be a big problem lately."

"Hitchhiking?"

"No, runaways. You guys are fortunate," Wilcox explained. "Most of these kids end up on the streets before they're apprehended—get exposed to all sorts of stuff, or worse. By the time the parents are brought into the picture, it's to come down to the morgue and make a positive ID."

The officer strode over to the cruiser, opened the door, and spoke firmly to Elise. "You can get out now. I'm gonna leave you in the custody of your parents." Elise didn't budge. The officer wasted no time in grabbing her arm and forcefully removing her from his cruiser—all the while instructing her harshly, "I don't have time for this foolishness. It's time to grow up. Face the music." He escorted her up to the doorway. "She's all yours."

"Thanks, Charlie. We'll handle the situation from here." Prescott nodded soberly, taking Elise's arm and steering her back into the house. "And I assure you, this won't happen again." He tightened his grip.

"Sorry I had to start your day off like this," Wilcox extended his apology while climbing back into his cruiser.

P r o g e n y

Neither Catherine nor Forrest responded to his comment; the massive mahogany doors had closed solidly behind them, the house seemingly swallowing them up.

The Letter

The sun had broken through the clouds, signaling an end to the dreariness of the last couple of days. The air felt invitingly warm, and Rachel welcomed the arrival of spring as she strolled down the walkway to retrieve the mail. Green had replaced the brown of winter, the foliage filling the empty spaces between tree branches. Neighboring houses could barely be seen through the trees, and azaleas—in full bloom—dotted the landscape with pink and white blossoms, forming a floral barrier along the front of the house. The dogwood blossoms had come and gone, and now the magnolias were poised for a spectacular display of white, fragrant blooms.

Rachel liked the sense of seclusion. What she didn't like was staying in bed so much. One more day of confinement seemed unbearable, and she looked forward to her daily jaunts to the mailbox. She knew Dr. MacKenzie's orders—take it easy and get plenty of rest—but this pregnancy didn't seem to be in jeopardy. She was almost six months, further along than any of her previous pregnancies. Definitely a good sign. Everything was moving along as expected, and even Matt seemed excited. Rachel had put her job on hold, with a promise to follow MacKenzie's instructions to the letter. She and Matt were deliberating over baby names—Duncan or Luke for a boy and Jenna or Leah for a girl. It was just so boring to be stuck at home, day after day.

As she flipped through the mail—magazines, circulars, letters, and bills—Rachel's eyes locked onto a creme envelope scrawled with unfamiliar handwriting: Mrs. Rachel Hamilton. *Who's writing me,* she wondered, expectantly turning it over. She gasped audibly as she read the engraved return address:

Elise Prescott
1132 Idlewild Blvd.
Downers Grove, Illinois

Not waiting to get back into the house, Rachel slowly lowered herself onto the weathered Wedgwood bench to the right of the walkway and set the stack of mail at her side. The mystery letter was her sole concern. Abandoning her usual ruthless approach to letter-opening, Rachel gently and methodically fingered the note, delicately pulling it from its envelope. The heavyweight, linenlike paper conveyed an understated elegance. Judging by what she'd seen of their house, it seemed fitting that correspondence from a Prescott would cast a polished, almost regal image. She opened the note, her eyes racing to assimilate its message:

Dear Mrs. Hamilton,

I'm sorry my mother and father were so rude the day you visited. I don't understand them or their attitudes, but they were talking about you when I came home from my field trip. When my father realized I was listening at the door, he turned white. I asked a few questions, and he got really mad. I couldn't understand his anger. I mean, what's the harm in asking questions? You do look like me—all my friends agree—and the old photo you left looks exactly like me.

Actually, it made me curious, too. I've never felt like I belonged in this family even though my counselor says it's normal for teenagers to feel this way. I tried to convince myself that my doubts were "all in my mind," as she keeps telling me, but the doubts just won't go away.

I'm writing to ask for your help. Our final biology project is to find out our parents' blood types and then trace our own type. My parents freaked out and refused to help me do my assignment. They said it wasn't any business of the school's. They even refused to tell *me* their blood types. I figured since you live in Chapel Hill, and that's where I was born, you could help me. Can you go to the hospital—N.C. Memorial—and find out my mother's blood type from records there? I know this is a crazy request, but I have to know the truth—not just for my assignment, but for me. I've also included a copy of my birth certificate. Please help me. I need to find out if this certificate is official and if they really are my parents.

It's strange to write to a woman I've never met. But I admire your persistence and feel special that someone would care enough to track me down. I'm sorry I didn't get to meet you when you were here. I think I would like you.

Sincerely,
Elise Prescott

It didn't take Rachel long to process the contents of the letter. Soon she had a plan in place, and disregarding doctor's orders, she ran back into the house. The kitchen phone was her immediate destination.

"Jenny, get over here fast. And bring a lab coat."

"Hold up, what are you talking about?"

"I got a letter, and you have to read it."

"From whom?"

"Come over and see for yourself. Hurry!"

"OK, but why the lab coat?"

"Just bring it!"

"All right. Be right there."

Rachel was waiting with the letter and the birth certificate in hand when Jenny rushed breathlessly through the back door with a lab coat draped over her arm. Rachel handed her the letter first. After a moment, an astonished Jenny looked up.

"No way! Did you write her? Matt will kill you."

"No. No. She contacted me."

"Well, you know what Matt said about having you admitted for a psych evaluation if you pursued this thing. Better drop it."

"But don't you see," Rachel pulled out the birth certificate, "Elise was born here—at Memorial, and Dr. Chan was the doctor. Don't you think that's too much of a coincidence?"

"Coincidence or not, Dr. Prescott really scared Matt

when he threatened to press harassment charges. You can't fool around with this."

"Look, I've been good. I didn't ask for this letter, but here it is."

"So Matt hasn't seen this?"

"No. Not yet. But I'm gonna show him as soon as I get the rest of the records."

"The rest of the records? What in the world are you planning?"

"Jenny, I have to follow up. I have to see the birth records."

"You're being irrational. Think about it. What good are birth records going to do? You already have a birth certificate. It's over. There's nothing left to find out."

"You don't understand. There's more. I feel it. Besides, there's this blood-type question that needs answering."

"Rachel, I'm not going to let you mess up your life. You and Matt are getting along better than ever. Don't jeopardize that."

"Getting along better because I don't bring up Elise or the dreams. I can't continue to pretend that it doesn't matter."

"Then think about this baby. Don't get caught up in something that will stress you out. You need to stay relaxed."

"You mean, I need to stay placated. Sorry, I can't do that. There's a connection here somewhere, and I'm gonna find it. Something happened fifteen years ago, and it wasn't a miscarriage!"

"Rachel!" Jenny's plea faded away as Rachel snatched the lab coat and disappeared out the door.

Rachel pulled her Volvo wagon into a space in the employee parking lot at Memorial. She slammed the car door, donned the lab coat, and headed toward the records room. Although beginning to show, she could still button the last button of the white overcoat. *Good. No one can tell I'm pregnant.* But even if they could tell, Rachel reminded herself, lots of pregnant women work at the hospital. No one would notice her. No one would think anything out of the ordinary.

The baby felt heavier than usual, but she convinced herself the walk to the basement wasn't that far. She could make it. Purposefully taking the side stairwell, Rachel hoped to avoid anyone she knew. Answering questions was the last thing she needed. Besides, she didn't want Matt hearing about her trip to the hospital.

Before reaching the record room entrance, Rachel pulled out Elise's birth certificate and reviewed it. Then, knowing it was imperative to look official, she checked to make sure Jenny's name tag was predominantly displayed:

Jennifer Sanderson, M.S.
Speech Pathologist

Rachel entered the room and casually approached the gray-haired matron bent over a computer terminal.

"I need the records pulled up on a patient—a Catherine Prescott." Rachel stated matter-of-factly.

"Can you spell that for me?"

"C–a–t–h–e–r–i–n–e P–r–e–s–c–o–t–t."

"I'll need the social security number," the woman said, barely lifting her head as she typed in the letters.

"How about a birth date?" Rachel countered, already prepared for the question.

"That'll work.."

"May 25, 1940."

The woman punched in a few numbers, then looked up. "The records aren't here. They're stored with the Clinical Research Unit files. Says they've been transferred to Biotech."

"You mean there's nothing there?" Rachel's heart sank.

"Just a lab workup, I guess they forgot to send it over."

"Can you print that out?"

"Sure, but I don't see how it's going to help you."

"Just give me what you've got. That'll be fine."

"Whatever." The woman dutifully pushed a few more keys.

Hmm . . . Biotech . . . there's that name again.

The printer produced several pages, which the woman tore off. "Here you go," she said, handing it over the countertop. "You'll have to sign here," she added, pushing a clipboard toward Rachel.

"Sure." Rachel folded the papers and shoved them into her pocket, then bent over and without thinking, signed her name instead of Jenny's. More focused on her outward demeanor than a successful scheme, she tried hard to maintain a cool and collected exterior, hoping the woman didn't notice her hands shaking. Her insides were churning, and she felt weak. Even so, she decided to ask one last thing. "Can you send for the rest of the chart?"

"I can put in a request for you. Can't promise anything."

"Just try. That would be very helpful. I'll check back later. Thanks."

Rachel turned and waddled towards the door. The heaviness was intensifying; it felt like she was carrying a bowling ball—not a baby—and even though sitting down was a strong impulse, she wasn't about to comply. She pushed onward, dragging herself back to the stairs and ignoring the mounting pressure as best she could. Panting and blowing as if participating in a childbirth class, she was determined to make it back to her car. Rachel grabbed the side railing at the foot of the stairs and began the long climb upward.

CHAPTER 11

Payback

Just as Matt predicted, reaching a consensus was proving not to be easy. After spending months hammering out a position statement on physician–assisted suicide, the ethics committee was still embroiled in controversy. Today was no exception. Matt knew the immediacy of the issue; the American Academy of Psychiatrists made sure of that. They needed an endorsement for a press release and had pressured him relentlessly to get the committee's response. Adopting it without dissent was the holdup.

"You guys think I'm gonna roll over and play dead on this one, but you're wrong." Dr. Andrew Macon's round face reddened as he lashed out at his colleagues. "You may think I'm just the token conservative whose voice doesn't count, but that won't keep me from exposing your built-in biases to the media."

"Oh, Andy, lighten up, don't be so paranoid." Fellow southerner Tom Hanson smiled broadly as he spoke, attempting to head off a routine collision between Macon and his committee counterpart, Dr. Joseph Halevi from Long Island.

"Yeah, Andy," the curly-headed Halevi cut in. "This is just a rough draft. The final resolution depends on input from everyone. No one's trying to coerce you into anything. Now's the time to raise your objections."

"You better believe I'll raise objections," Macon continued. "Do you realize Hitler's final solution started with the medical profession? Killing psychiatric patients and handicapped children started with department heads in academic medicine. Doctors were gassing psychiatric patients in fake shower rooms before the Nazis even thought of it."

"Hold on," stormed Halevi, indignantly shaking his head. "Now you're calling us Nazis? Someone put this man out of his misery. He's crazy!"

"I'm just saying we have to be awfully careful not to set the same vehicle in motion." Macon's voice broke off as he monitored the faces around the conference table for signs of agreement.

"And what might that vehicle be?" Halevi rolled his eyes at the others, amused with his line of questioning which only served to string Macon along.

"Playing God." Macon spoke with conviction. "The Declaration of Geneva reaffirmed the Hippocratic tradition, maintaining respect for life from the time of conception. Didn't you recite the oath at your med school graduation, Halevi?" Macon was off on a tangent now, recounting the oath out loud: "'I will not use my medical knowledge contrary to the laws of humanity.'"

Hanson interrupted the recitation. "Calm down, Andy. We're not the enemy. And you know we aren't supposed to bring up the God stuff."

"I can't leave God out." Macon pounded his fist on the table. "Killing patients is a moral issue, and this compassion nonsense doesn't make it right. I won't let you put me in a box. My religious views are the only way out of this insanity."

"Want to talk about insanity?" Halevi was ready to do battle. "Let's talk about the Crusades, the Salem Witchcraft trials, Jim Jones, and David Koresh. Come on, let's get it all out!"

"OK guys, time-out," Matt signed a *T* with his hands. "Let's get back on task." He had seen these heated discussions go on forever without any resolution and knew it was time to pull rank. Out of respect for his friend, he offered a conciliatory remark; "Andy makes a good point. We should all be concerned about setting a precedent . . . a destructive precedent." He nodded toward Halevi. "Please make a note of that in the resolution."

Despite Matt's attempt at peacemaking, the tension hung in the air like secondhand smoke, and no one budged. They were waiting for Macon's reaction, as it was unlike him to dismiss the subject without a fight. Halevi in particular was poised to strike at the first sign of resistance. But Macon surprised them all by hurling no accusations, firing off no objections.

Two raps on the paneled conference room door provided a welcome diversion. The door squeaked open, and a fair-haired head peered around the edge. A timid little woman asked hesitantly, "Dr. Hamilton?"

"Yes," Matt answered.

"There's been an accident . . . your wife . . . they called from the ER."

Stunned silence penetrated the room. No one said a word. Matt jumped to his feet, fumbled around his chair, and made his way to the doorway. As an afterthought to properly disengage from the meeting, he cocked his head over his shoulder and said in a detached manner, "Carry on. Catch me up on the details." His voice trailed off as he exited the room.

Matt didn't bother calling the ER. He escaped the psych wing through a side door to the nearest stairwell and bounded down three flights in about thirty seconds. Darting around corners, ducking in and out of office areas, crossing through waiting rooms and hallways, Matt took the well-worn shortcuts and halved the time it usually took to go from one end of the hospital to the other.

The ER conveyed an air of controlled chaos. Accustomed to the continual flow of personnel in and out of the ER, the triage nurse wasn't startled when Matt appeared seemingly out of nowhere. Her face registered a look of recognition, and without blinking an eye, she said, "They've taken her to labor and delivery." On cue, he turned and headed toward the delivery suite. No time to exchange pleasantries.

The baby . . . we're gonna lose the baby . . . oh, please God, not again.

Matt's adrenalin was pumping. The fear of losing this baby consumed him. Never had he cared so much about Rachel and their future. Never before had his work taken second place to thoughts of a family. Things were falling into place for the first time, and he considered this pregnancy to be the fresh start they desperately needed.

No, no. It can't end like this. I won't let it.

Dr. Judith MacKenzie met Matt as he entered the labor and delivery waiting room area and walked with him toward room 5, the obstetrical OR. "We've got her prepped and ready to go. We may lose the baby, and we won't know about the mother's condition for at least 24 hours." She relayed the information as if she were making rounds, giving a report to a fellow physician.

"What happened?"

"I'm sorry. I thought you knew." MacKenzie's expression changed from somber to sympathetic; from clinically objective to supportive friend. "Who have you talked with?"

"No one. I came straight to the ER, and they sent me over here."

"Well, all I know is that Rachel ran a red light and was hit broadside—head injury. Don't know how bad it is, but she's unconscious now and in premature labor. Got to do an emergency C-section, the baby's breech."

"What are the baby's chances?"

"I figure Rachel's around 23, 24 weeks. If the baby's strong, there is a possibility she could make it. It depends."

"On what?"

"Whether there was trauma associated with the accident, lung development, birth weight. We'll just have to wait and see." MacKenzie threw her hands up, indicating an unpredictable outcome.

When they reached the obstetrical OR, MacKenzie stopped at the door and turned toward Matt. "I know this isn't the birth experience you planned on, but you're welcome to scrub in if you wish."

"OK. . . . Give me a minute. . . ."

MacKenzie responded to the strained look on Matt's face. "It's alright to be the concerned husband and father; you don't have to play the role of doctor at the same time. Just take it easy. I've got everything under control." She gave his arm a reassuring squeeze and then pushed the buzzer to open

134

the doors. "Go sit down. It'll take a few minutes before we're ready to start." The doors swung open, and Dr. MacKenzie disappeared into the inner sanctum.

Matt stood dumbfounded. Paralysis set in. His head said, "Follow MacKenzie," but his heart stopped him. He didn't understand the hesitation. Here they were preparing to bring his child into the world, yet he couldn't even bring himself to walk through those doors. What was holding him back? He propped himself up against the cold, stark-white wall. Avoidance was the coward's way out. He knew it. But facing reality was more than he could handle right now. He closed his eyes for a moment. . . .

———————————

"Dr. Hamilton. . . . " Someone broke into his thoughts. Matt snapped to attention. A nurse, dressed in a pink scrub dress, took him by the arm and led him down the hallway. "Your baby has been taken to the intensive care nursery. They've incubated her, and she's on a ventilator. You can see her now, if you wish." They made their way through the maze into another waiting area, stopping at the entrance to the intensive care nursery. "You'll need to scrub up first." She pointed toward the sinks on the side wall. Matt still couldn't speak. This was about a baby. His baby. Small and weak . . . connected to life support. He didn't know if he was ready to deal with it.

"Dr. Hamilton, what are you doing down here?" Dr. Saldana quizzed, obviously surprised to see him. Matt recognized Saldana as the new Hopkins-trained neonatologist but had never spoken to him personally.

"My baby's in here." Matt answered in a shaky voice.

"Hamilton . . . the new admission. That's why I'm here. Come with me."

Matt put himself on automatic pilot and followed Dr. Saldana's lead, going through the hand-washing ritual and donning a gown. They walked through the unit, past rocking chairs and mothers standing beside isolettes with hands through the portholes, gently stroking their babies. There was an array of sights and sounds: bright overhead lamps lighting up the unit; nurses scurrying about checking vital signs and turning off alarms; lab techs drawing blood and maneuvering X-ray machinery into tight spaces; individual infant monitors blinking and beeping as they measured heart rate, respiration, and blood pressure. Almost all the babies were hooked to IVs administering fluids.

In the far corner, they approached a tablelike bed positioned under a warmer. A team of pink-clad individuals were working on a baby, attaching electronic leads, and starting an IV. A. card taped above the bed designated personhood:

BABY GIRL HAMILTON
992 GRAMS

Matt felt his legs buckling involuntarily as his eyes rested on the tiny, seemingly lifeless body engulfed in wires and tubing. Dr. Saldana merged with the activity around the bed but Matt pulled back, grabbing a nearby stool to support his faltering body, and then seated himself outside the work crew's way.

Suddenly, reality hit full force. This child, this helpless, vulnerable baby was about the same size as the one Chan—he stopped short of thinking the unthinkable. But think it or not, say it or not, the fact remained. He slumped down, suddenly overcome with guilt. He held his head in his hands, retreating into his thoughts. Years of deceiving Rachel seemed minor compared to the realization of what he had allowed to happen to his first child. What kind of father would actively promote the destruction of his own flesh and blood? Where was the instinct to protect? He wanted to pray but was afraid. Would God listen to him? No. Not now, not after what he'd done. *This is payback,* he thought. *I deserve whatever happens. . . .*

———————

Sitting next to Rachel's motionless form, resting his forehead on her hand, Matt acknowledged he had no control over the events unfolding before him. And although the nurse's instructions to "sound hopeful" seemed futile, Matt tried anyway. "Rachel, we have a daughter. You need to wake up so we can name her."

He had followed those orders for the last eight hours, and there had been no change in her condition. No response whatsoever. Matt wondered if Rachel could even hear him. Disillusionment set in. Who was he kidding? He didn't know how long they would have a daughter or if he would even get his wife back. No one could give him answers. The grave uncertainty of the situation made him feel like he was participating in a charade. Of course he was relieved that Rachel had made it through surgery and was now under observation in the I.C.U. It was just so awkward. The little cubicles provided very little privacy, and Matt felt conspicuous. He was "Dr. Hamilton," and being on the patient side of things generated a helpless feeling—a feeling unfamiliar to him. Paranoia struck. Everyone—nurses, lab technicians, other physicians—seemed to be watching his every move. Could they tell? Could they see *guilt* stamped across his forehead?

But they weren't his chief concern. Rachel, how would Rachel react if she knew the truth? Unable to contain his emotions any longer, Matt clutched Rachel's arm and buried his head into the sheets, tears streaming from his eyes. "Oh, Rachel, I'm so sorry. Can you ever forgive me?" His body shook as the grief poured out.

The whole ordeal, starting with Rachel's emergency surgery, had drained Matt emotionally and physically. He wanted to collapse, right there on the spot, but he knew he couldn't. He straightened up, marshaled his strength, and regained control of himself. Surely a strong guy like himself could handle the situation. What would the nurses think if he gave way to the emotional forces pulling him down? He must maintain an outward facade of composure. . . .

"Matt." A strong hand pressed on his shoulder. Matt lifted his eyes to see a concerned Andy Macon standing alongside him.

"Andy! What are you doing here?"

"It's late, almost midnight. I was worried about you. I'll bet you haven't left Rachel's side all day, haven't even gotten a bite to eat."

"Well, no . . . but I'm . . . not hungry," Matt stuttered.

Eating was the farthest thing from his mind. He stood up, focusing on the gold-rimmed glasses perched atop Andy's nose. People could say a lot of things about Macon's views, but they sure couldn't say he wasn't compassionate. Matt stared at him in amazement, not understanding why Macon would care about him. Matt had never done anything to deserve his concern. It was puzzling.

"I've come to see that you get home. Get some rest and nourishment. Doctor's orders you know."

"I can't leave. What if Rachel comes to?"

"Then they'll call you. You have a beeper, remember? Come on, I'll treat you to a sandwich in the cafeteria." He clasped Matt's elbow and gently guided him out of the unit.

Matt was too tired to protest. Besides, it was nice to have someone else making the decisions for a change. Macon ordered a BLT, chips, and a cup of coffee for Matt, and they sat in silence as Matt consumed his meal.

"Listen," Macon was the first to speak. "I'm gonna send Sally over with a couple of casseroles. You can just stick them in the microwave."

"That's not necessary. Too much trouble."

"No trouble at all. Sally's known as the Casserole Queen at church—always got 'em frozen and ready to go on a moment's notice. We'll just drop them by, sometime tomorrow?"

Matt nodded in compliance.

"Now, we need to get you home." Macon steered Matt along toward the cafeteria door, announcing, "We're outta here," to no one in particular.

CHAPTER 12

Connections

The mental fog was beginning to lift. It had been a week since the accident, and Matt was settling into a routine; alternating visits between the intensive care nursery and Rachel's room. Rachel was still under observation but had been transferred from I.C.U. to a room on a medical floor in the neurological wing. Her new surroundings offered some degree of privacy, and Matt no longer felt as if he were on display.

"Morning Babe." Matt's greeting signaled his entrance into Rachel's room. He dragged a chair over to her bedside, then leaned over and kissed her cheek, not expecting a response. Having grown accustomed to conversing in a one-way fashion, Matt began his daily report. "I just came from seeing our daughter. She's not out of the dark yet, but it looks promising. Still holding at 2 pounds 3 ounces, and she's taking more breaths on her own. But she really needs her mother . . . thought you'd like to know."

He sat his cup of coffee on the bedside table and spread out the morning paper across her bed, now part of his routine. "Let's see what's in the news today." Matt scanned the paper for something of interest for Rachel, but a second page headline abruptly ended his search: "Biotech Global Operations in Jeopardy." He read on:

> Dr. Robert Chan, a scientist for Biotechnologies Research International located in Research Triangle Park, will testify before the Senate Foreign Relations committee today in Washington, D.C. as Senator Peter Holmes (R-NC) probes further into human rights violations and current trade agreements with China. If the subcommittee fails to recommend granting favored nation status to China, Chan's international research collaborations could be affected.

Matt's body tensed. Chan's very name evoked a visceral

response. Although he'd lost all contact with the man after he left the university, Matt's blood was boiling. Just what was Chan up to? Did Holmes know what kind of man Chan was? Did he know about Chan's Chinese partners? Matt grit his teeth as the events of the preceding week flashed before him. He needed someone to blame, a focal point for his anguish. Chan easily qualified.

"Heeeyyy, Matt." A southern drawl broke the silence. "Thought I'd find you here." Andy Macon's wide grin brightened the room as he strolled in, hands stuck in his pockets.

Matt slowly reoriented himself. "Oh, Andy . . . I'm glad you dropped by. Wanted to thank you for the food. Tell Sally her chicken-rice casserole was great."

"Glad to help out. How are things here?" he glanced toward Rachel.

"About the same."

"And the baby?"

"Holding on . . . no setbacks."

"Good to hear. . . ." Macon shuffled his feet nervously. "So, how are *you* doing?"

"Fine." Matt quickly fired off his answer. But since he wasn't up for psychoanalysis, he quickly diverted the conversation to something less threatening. He reached over, picked up the newspaper, then looked squarely into Andy's eyes. "What do you know about Biotech and Dr. Chan?"

"Pardon me?" Macon's face registered a puzzled expression.

"This article. Haven't you read today's paper?"

"Well, no, but I do know about Dr. Chan. Er, Dr. Robert Chan?"

"Yes." Matt wasn't surprised Macon knew Chan. Macon always had information on controversial issues. Problem was, no one usually wanted to hear it. Today, Matt broke rank. "What do you know?"

"Just that Chan is an evil man. Unscrupulous."

"Wanna give me specifics?"

"He's been dealing in abortions for quite awhile. Notorious for his D and X procedure. I've even picketed his research facility."

"This research facility, exactly what's that all about?"

"You don't know? He experiments on fetal tissue, the brain, the pancreas—you name it. Big money from the National Institutes of Health and private corporations."

"Is that legal?"

"Of course it is. The president vetoed the ban on fetal tissue research. Where have you been?"

"Just not interested, I guess. Where does he get the tissue?"

"Boy, you *are* in the dark!" Macon's voice cracked. His eyes flashed fire.

"OK, OK. I admit I'm out of touch with this issue, but settle down. No need to get all bent out of shape."

"Well, why did you bring up Chan in the first place?"

"This article mentioned him," Matt waved the newspaper in front of him. "And, um, I used to work for him . . .

but—" Matt hesitated. "I never knew all this."

"You mean you didn't want to know," Macon huffed in disgust. "Like most people, you'd rather stick your head in the sand."

Ignoring his tendency to get his hackles up in defense, Matt redirected the conversation. "Why do you think Chan is testifying about trade with China?"

"Probably wants to keep his buddies over there in business."

"What business?" Even though Matt had his own ideas about Chan's operation, he wanted to hear someone else's viewpoint.

"Don't know exactly, but I can guess. Probably has something to do with fetal tissue research. Regardless, their mandatory one child policy translates into forced abortions, so as far as I'm concerned, they don't deserve favored nation status. Period."

"But why would China import fetal tissue if they perform all those abortions? Sounds like they have enough tissue of their own."

"Can't answer you there. I just know that the Chinese government has zero respect for human life. They sanction sick stuff."

"Like what?"

"Marketing human body parts on the black market and executing political prisoners to supply transplant organs for their deals.

"I find that hard to believe."

"Hey, that's nothing. They consider fetuses a delicacy, eat 'em for health reasons."

"That's disgusting!"

"Disgusting or not, it's true. Major media won't touch it though. Too gruesome."

"You're right on that one. No one would believe it. . . . I sure don't."

"It really doesn't matter what you believe. Refusing to believe something doesn't make it any less real. But at least they're consistent."

"Consistent?"

"Yeah, in their regard for life. Their policies didn't come out of nowhere, you know. Look at past actions, like in the '60s when they ate the corpses of counterrevolutionaries to show loyalty to Mao. It's a pattern."

"Enough already!" Matt shook his head in disgust. "I'm sorry I even brought this up. Just drop it."

"OK, but you have to understand one thing: people who understand the connection between China and Chan are outraged, and if someone doesn't stop him legally, no telling what will happen."

"You mean someone will bomb his research facility?" There was a hint of sarcasm in his voice.

"Matt, don't make light of this. There's a lot of righteous anger out there. Strong motives to eliminate Chan from the picture."

Strong motives? Eliminate Chan? The thought sent a chill down Matt's spine. He turned ashen. An awkward moment of silence passed as Matt reflected on Andy's comment. Suddenly Macon apologized. "Sorry, I shouldn't have gotten off on this. I really wanted to talk about you."

"It's OK. I brought it up." Matt detached himself from the conversation. His words were mechanical now. "Besides, I'm running late. Got to get over to the office." Not waiting for a reply, he hurried out, leaving Macon standing with a baffled look on his face.

When Matt reached his office, the receptionist met him at the entrance, announcing, "Dr. Hamilton, a registered letter just arrived. I signed for you." She handed over a white 8 x 10 postal envelope and then proceeded to rattle off Matt's schedule for the day, all the while racing to keep pace with his long strides. "I put the rest of your mail on your desk. There's also an ethics committee memo." She stopped to catch her breath as Matt paused in the doorway to his office. Then she added, "And don't forget about tonight's dinner meeting."

"OK, OK, got it covered." Matt, anxious to see what was in the envelope, turned to go into his office.

"Oh yes, Halevi wants to talk with you before the meeting."

"Fine. Tell him to meet me in front of the Health Sciences building at 5:00—after my lecture. He can walk with me up to the Carolina Inn."

She nodded in compliance.

"Give me a minute before sending in my first appointment." Matt smiled appreciatively, then shut the door, made his way to his desk, and ripped open the envelope as he sank down into a leather swivel chair. The letterhead jumped out as if to say, "Make the connection":

Biotechnologies Research International

Corporate Offices, Downers Grove, Illinois

Forrest Prescott, Ph.D, Director of Operations

Although Matt vaguely remembered the police officer from Downers Grove mentioning Prescott's affiliation with Biotech, he had never made the connection until now. Matt's thoughts were racing as he read the letter.

Dr. Hamilton:

I am writing on behalf of my clients, Dr. Forrest Prescott and his family, to give you and your wife notice that you shall have no further contact with the Prescotts, either directly or indirectly. Your pursuit of Elise Prescott and the unauthorized request for Mrs. Prescott's medical records has been alarming to the family. Dr. Prescott is prepared to take whatever civil or criminal action may be required to ensure that his privacy and the privacy of his family are maintained. If any such proceedings were instituted, your wife's history of mental instability could certainly become an issue. I trust you understand the seriousness of this matter and that you and your wife will govern yourselves accordingly.

Sincerely,
Jeffrey R. Taggett, esq.

What? Rachel requested medical records? Her undaunted quest amazed him, but he knew she had crossed the line this time. Nevertheless, Matt was growing weary of Prescott's legal maneuvering. His lawyer had already called once—after Rachel's trip to Chicago—wanting to make sure Matt was aware of the gravity of the situation. It wasn't just an idle threat either. What was Doctor Prescott trying to hide? And why the excessive concern over privacy? Matt mentally dictated a reply:

Dear Dr. Prescott,
You will be pleased to know that Rachel is no longer a threat to your world—not in her present condition. She's in a coma. However, I appreciate the information about Rachel's activities. Perhaps I'll discover what she was up to when she wakes up.

Sincerely,
Matt Hamilton

Matt wondered if Prescott knew why Rachel wanted his wife's medical records. Had she found out something new about Elise? Maybe that's what Prescott's lawyer was alluding to. Regardless, Matt knew he was responsible for setting the whole scenario in motion and that fact cut deep into his conscience. Memories of the first miscarriage surfaced, and the guilty verdict replayed once more: Rachel would never have been injured if she hadn't been searching for a mystery girl—a mystery girl invented to compensate for the loss of a real daughter. But was it a daughter? How could he know? How could anyone know? It was a disturbing question.

Halevi was waiting on a concrete bench as Matt emerged from the Health Sciences building. He jumped up and matched Matt's stride. Although his smile seemed genuine enough, Matt suspected he was there for more than a friendly stroll. His thick Long Island accent, unaffected by years in the south, distinctly set him apart. "So, what was your class on today?"

"Bipolar disorders."

"And who were the recipients of that vast storehouse of knowledge?"

"The usual—medical students." Matt offered no details, frustrating Halevi and forcing him to keep the conversation going on his own.

"So, what's the status with Rachel?"

"Nothing new." Again, Matt didn't elaborate; he just didn't trust Halevi's motives for asking. It wasn't like Halevi to keep up with Matt's personal life, and besides, Matt thought, he didn't even know Rachel. Not really. Matt chuckled as he remembered Rachel's assessment: "Halevi really thinks he's something, doesn't he? What's with the gold chain around his neck anyway? Am I supposed to be impressed?"

"Something funny?" Halevi quizzed, noting Matt's self-absorption.

"No . . . just thinking about something Rachel once said."

Silence filled the void.

Matt wasn't participating in the social exchange, and Halevi got the message loud and clear. He wasted no further time, quickly cutting to the point. "I've been doing some thinking, Matt. The committee is going to have a hard time pulling together a position statement as long as Macon is around."

"Your point?"

"Isn't there some way we can have him assigned to another committee? Get him to chair it or something?"

"You know as well as I do that we were all appointed for a reason, and we're stuck with one another. Live with it."

"Yeah, but his right-wing fanaticism only complicates things. I hear he's been testifying on Capitol Hill. Isn't that a conflict of interest?"

"I'm aware of the Capitol Hill issue, and it has nothing to do with what we're working on. You'll have to come up with a better angle than that." Matt spoke definitively; refusing to give Halevi an inch. Without a point to argue, Halevi didn't push the subject further. They stopped at Columbia Street, waited for the light to change, then crossed over, and walked up the hill towards the Carolina Inn. As they approached the side entrance, Macon stepped out of the shadows and eyed the two physicians suspiciously. Then he waved several papers toward Matt. "I found the China article for you. I knew I had it somewhere."

Halevi broke in, shaking his head, "Don't tell me, now you're on a rampage against the Chinese. It's always something isn't it?" Halevi didn't expect a response, he just wanted to verbalize his disdain for Macon and his causes.

"Listen, Joe," Macon spoke gingerly. "I don't want to argue with you, not now, not tonight. Can't we call a truce?"

"Don't know what calling a truce will do. We're at opposite ends of the spectrum on just about everything. Controversy is inevitable."

"But it shouldn't be. You of all people should understand where I'm coming from."

"I'm not following you, Andy. But then, that's not unusual."

"I'm talking about our worldviews. They should be similar."

"Worldview?"

152

"You know, how we view life . . . why we're here on this planet . . . what happens when we die. . . ."

"Are you saying we hold similar philosophies? Not a chance, Macon."

"You're Jewish aren't you?" Macon's voice was rising.

"So? Got a problem with that?"

"Joe. Stop and think for just one moment. Think about why you believe the way you do. There's a starting point for everything, and yours is inconsistent with where you're ending up."

"Macon, this is going nowhere. Give it up. I don't have the foggiest idea what you're getting at."

"Just stay with me a minute . . . your Jewish heritage— what did it teach you about the value of life?"

"I don't know," Halevi replied wearily.

"Why is man special? Why is he different from the animals?" Macon paused for a response. Getting nothing, he continued. "Isn't it because we're made in God's image? Isn't that what gives life meaning?"

"According to you, maybe."

"No, according to the Judeo-Christian tradition, beginning with *your* tradition. Are you willing to throw out the convictions held for centuries, convictions that have held civilization together, and replace them with pagan philosophies which devalue human life?"

Halevi didn't respond.

"Don't you see what happens?" Macon pleaded.

Halevi shrugged his shoulders.

"Death on demand!"

Again, no response from Halevi. He had completely disengaged.

Matt took advantage of the opportunity and jumped in. "Hey guys, let's move on. If we don't get in there and get started with the meeting, we'll never finish."

Despite Matt's skillful closure, Macon wouldn't let it go. He disregarded Matt and pleaded once more with Halevi. "I want you to understand. It's what Hitler was all about. He decided the Jews didn't count. He said they were less than human. See the connection? See?"

"Macon! Enough. Halevi isn't interested."

Matt didn't relish the thought of conducting tonight's skirmish; mediating between Halevi and Macon was going to be strained at best. All Matt really wanted to do was be with Rachel. That was his objective. The sooner he could get through the ethics meeting, the sooner he'd be with Rachel. Nothing else really mattered.

CHAPTER 13

Wake-up Call

The chase was on. She was running again, eluding some sinister force, protecting a baby. This time she was in a church, the church she had grown up in. It didn't make sense. Shouldn't this be a safe haven? Shouldn't she find protection here? Unfortunately not. This was no refuge. She must hide. Quickly.

Except for Rachel and her assailants, the building was empty. She vaulted up the stairs and entered a plushly carpeted room with velvet curtains. A round table, covered with a floor-length tapestry, was the only place to hide. As the footsteps grew closer, she crawled beneath the table, hoping to evade her pursuers. She huddled quietly, trying to still her shaking body, afraid even to breathe. She clutched the child tightly. What if the baby cried out, revealing their hideout? She couldn't take the chance. Impulsively, she burst forth from beneath the table, catching a glimpse of a man wielding a knife.

The next moment she found herself leaping from the sanctuary door into the street, convincing herself she would find a policeman. But the street was empty. No cars. No help in sight. She quickened her step. Desperation filled her soul. Someone please be there! Someone save the baby! They were after the baby, she knew that now. "Help me, help me . . . someone help me . . ."

"Mrs. Hamilton, calm down." A nurse wiped the perspiration from Rachel's brow and brushed her damp, tangled hair away from her face. The comatose patient had been restless all morning, writhing around in the bed, fighting against the confines of the bedsheets. This was the first time she had spoken audibly since her accident. Now she was crying out for help from a semiconscious state.

Suddenly, Rachel's eyes opened into a wide-eyed stare. She sat straight up, grabbed the nurse's arm, and cried out again, "Help me!"

"Mrs. Hamilton, you're in the hospital. You're safe." The nurse attempted to console her confused, frightened patient.

Slowly and cautiously, Rachel looked around. Even though the sunshine glaring through the blinds made her squint, she could clearly see she was in a hospital room: the nurse in white, a bedside table, an eating tray, even a television mounted on the wall. The antiseptic smell registered familiar, and in the distance she could hear an overhead page, "Dr. Wilton. Please call the operator, Dr. Gerald Wilton." What a relief to be awake. And safe. She loosed her grip on the nurse's arm. Slowly the memory of what happened returned. "I crashed."

"Yes, Mrs. Hamilton. You ran a red light."

"My baby . . . ." Rachel's hands glided across the flat surface of her abdomen, and immediately her sense of peace vanished. "My baby! They took my baby!" For a moment she thought she was still dreaming. *Oh, let this be a nightmare. Please let this be a nightmare!*

"Settle down, Mrs. Hamilton. Your baby is in the intensive care nursery."

Could she believe her? Was the nurse part of the

conspiracy? Something snapped inside, and horror took control. Rachel screamed hysterically.

"No, no you can't have my baby. Give my baby back!" The nurse tried to restrain her, but Rachel was fighting now, fighting mad and determined to get out of bed. "You can't do this to me. I have to find my baby. Let me go!"

Rachel struggled as another nurse entered the room and injected a medication into the IV connected to her arm. Rachel continued to struggle while the first nurse held her down until the room and everything in it began to fade.

"Rachel, Rachel. It's Matt. You're OK now."

Still sedated, Rachel could hear Matt's voice and feel the warmth of his breath against her ear. He was sitting on the edge of the bed, encircling her with his strong arms and offering reassuring words. "I'm sorry I wasn't here when you woke up. We have a baby girl, a daughter." Not expecting a response, he continued whispering, "The baby's fine. You can't go psycho on me. Please believe me. She's OK."

Rachel's body softened in his arms. Matt's presence alone provided the reassurance she needed. She forced open her heavy eyelids and saw Matt's blurred figure leaning over her. He was searching her eyes for a hint of understanding, a hint of recognition. Words would not form on her lips, so she smiled weakly and responded with her eyes. *Of course I believe you. You've never given me reason not to.* He kissed her tenderly on the forehead, and Rachel closed her eyes once more. Ah, to relax. Matt was in control.

The lights were out when Rachel awoke again. The night shift had taken over, and hospital activity was at a low. Matt was still there, asleep in a chair pulled up close to her bed, his head propped up with several pillows. "Matt," she whispered, "I'm awake."

His eyes shot open. "Rachel!"

"Darling, I need to see my daughter."

Matt straightened up and checked his watch. "It's late, it's after midnight."

"I have to see her—now. You've got to take me." There was a sense of urgency in her voice, and Matt knew not to press the issue.

"OK. Let me find a wheelchair." He disappeared into the darkness.

Rachel could hardly contain her excitement. She had a daughter . . . a real daughter . . . her own flesh and blood. Tears welled up in her eyes. *Oh, dear God, don't let this end.*

Rachel stared down at the fragile, tiny baby that everyone referred to as her daughter. This was not what she expected. No one had prepared her for what she saw. Matt had simply instructed her how to scrub up, then wheeled her next to a tablelike bed and helped seat her on the stool beside it. No warning whatsoever. He never bothered to comment on the baby's condition or size. Now, beneath a mesh of tubes and wires, lay her daughter, an infant so small she would fit in a shoe box. Rachel felt nothing. No maternal warmth, no sense of ownership. She couldn't even make eye contact.

"I know she looks small, but trust me," a nurse smiled as she offered encouragement. "We're very encouraged with how well she's doing. She's a real fighter." Then as if anticipating her questions, the nurse began explaining. "The tube in her throat prevents her from crying. It will be awhile before she is able to breathe completely on her own. Then we'll take her off the machine."

Rachel did not enter into a conversation with this nurse. She was frozen, her eyes fixated on a fat syringe filled with blood, connected by tubing into the umbilical cord. Several doctors stood around the bed, so intent on their procedure that they were oblivious to Rachel's and Matt's presence.

The nurse, noticing Rachel's startled expression, continued her explanations. "Don't let the blood frighten you. We're just replacing some of her blood with a fresh supply. It's routine. Nothing to be concerned about."

The words did not provide comfort. Rachel looked

away, searching for another focal point. Her eyes rested on a bag of fluids slowly infusing into the limp, little body. The drip, drip, drip of the infusion pump lulled her into a quasi-hypnotic trance. As she stared fixedly, she could hear Dr. MacKenzie's explanation about blood incompatibility in her mind: *Sometimes the mother's body makes antibodies against the baby's blood if it is different from her own. They attack the baby's blood cells.*

"Is there a blood incompatibility problem with my baby?" Rachel finally spoke up.

"Oh no. She just has too much bilirubin in her system. We're doing an exchange."

"Bili . . . ?" Rachel looked puzzled.

"Bili-ru-bin," the nurse sounded it out. "It's caused by the normal breakdown of red blood cells. It's just that a preemie has a harder time filtering it because the liver isn't mature enough."

"Oh. But how did you know she had too much bil-i-ru-bin?" Rachel tried to pronounce it correctly.

"We drew a little blood, then sent it to the lab. They analyzed it and sent back a lab report. Pretty standard stuff. Your baby's going to be fine."

Rachel nodded as if the nurse had answered her unspoken question. However, she wasn't thinking about her baby. She was thinking about another lab report, the lab report she had retrieved from the record room. She had not forgotten. Was it still in her lab coat? What had it said? She must check.

"Matt, I feel weak. Can you take me back to the room now?"

"Sure. I should have known this was too much too soon."

"I'm fine. I just need to rest now." Rachel plopped down in the wheelchair and waited for Matt to push her.

"Mrs. Hamilton?" the nurse posed a question. "Have you named her?"

Rachel looked at Matt for an answer, but an empty look was all she got. She turned back to the nurse and answered apologetically, "We haven't had time."

"That's all right. No rush. We'd just like to call her by name. Let us know as soon as you name her. OK?"

"OK," Rachel replied feebly. She felt like she was living out a dream or at least was outside of her body watching the whole scene from a distance. It was weird.

"Please come visit again. In the morning. Your daughter needs you . . . needs to hear your voice."

"I know," Rachel said halfheartedly. Of course the nurse was right, but how was she supposed to manufacture feelings for this child? How could she do "mother" things when she didn't even feel like this child's mother?

The nurse noted Rachel's apprehension and offered a parting bit of wisdom. "Just give it some time. Things will be better tomorrow."

"Thank you," Rachel said politely. She waved an uncertain good-bye as Matt wheeled her around and steered her out of the unit.

The sun's glare greeted Rachel the moment she opened her eyes. The breakfast tray sat untouched, and she realized she had slept through most of the morning. Still somewhat groggy, she replayed yesterday's events, recalling the late-night visit to the I.C.N. and her conversation with Matt into the early morning hours. This was the first chance she'd had to follow up on the lab report. She purposely failed to mention it to Matt, knowing he probably couldn't handle hearing how she got it; she must wait until all the details came together.

But where was her lab coat, the clothes she was wearing the day of the accident? Had Matt taken them home? She reached for the call button and rang for the nurse.

A few moments passed before anyone responded. Then suddenly, the door flew open and a stocky nurse in a white pantsuit breezed into the room.

"Good morning, Mrs. Hamilton. So glad you decided to join the waking world. I understand you came to while I was off yesterday, then had to be sedated. Are you OK today?"

"Much better—once I got to see my daughter."

"Great. So what can I do for you now?"

"My clothes and things, where would they be?"

"I'm not sure. You came here from the intensive care

unit. I assume they put your things in a plastic bag and gave them to your husband, or . . ." She opened the door of the bedside table. "They put them in here." She pulled out a bag and handed it to Rachel, who had pulled herself to a sitting position on the edge of the bed, her tummy still sore from surgery.

"Thanks." Rachel said, peering inside and breathing a sigh of relief at the sight of the lab coat.

"Anything else I can get for you?" the nurse asked.

"Oh, no. Just glad to find my things."

"OK then. I'm going to page Dr. MacKenzie. She asked to be notified when you woke up this morning. So did the neurologist. Seems everyone wants to talk. Try to eat some of your breakfast, a muffin or something. You need the strength." The nurse positioned the breakfast tray in front of Rachel, then turned and exited the room.

Rachel anxiously retrieved a bloodstained lab coat from the bag, encouraged to find the lab report still safely folded in the pocket just as she had left it. She pulled it out and began perusing it, trying to make sense of the numbers and medical abbreviations as she took a bite out of the pear she found on her tray.

"I hear you finally decided to wake up," Dr. MacKenzie teased as she waltzed into Rachel's room. "You know you really overdid it after your accident—a nap is one thing, but this Rip Van Winkle act was a bit much."

Rachel looked up and grinned but didn't try to offer a

defense. Over the preceding months, MacKenzie had become more than an obstetrician to her, more like a close friend. "So you're saying I've missed a lot?"

"Just your daughter's birth. Nothing important," MacKenzie flashed one of her warm, radiant smiles. "Seriously though, Matt impressed everyone with his vigilance. Hardly ever left your side. He obviously loves you a lot."

"It's nice to hear that; he's never been very verbal. I have to take what I can get, whenever I can."

"Well, store up the image of Matt sitting by your side, holding your hand, and talking to an unresponsive wife day after day. You just may need to remember that."

"OK, I get the message. Everyone loves Matt around here. No one likes to see him hurting. But what about me, don't I get any sympathy?"

"Sure. You know I'm just playing with your mind," MacKenzie chuckled.

"Speaking of minds, mind if I tap into yours?" Rachel waved the report in front of MacKenzie's face. "I need help deciphering this lab report."

MacKenzie took it from her hand and began reviewing it, then stopped and gave Rachel a puzzled look. "This isn't yours. Whose is this?"

"No one you know. I'm trying to unravel a mystery. What can you tell me about this person from the results there?"

MacKenzie studied the report carefully, her eyebrows knitted together as she read. Then she shook her head. "This doesn't make sense. It's really strange."

"What?" Rachel leaned forward.

"For one thing, the mom's blood type is O positive and the baby is AB."

"What's the possibility that a type O mother could have a type AB child?"

"None."

"What do you mean 'none'?"

"Just what I said, 'none.'"

"Well, what if the father was AB, could the child be AB then?"

"Not a chance. If the father was AB, he could only give up an A or B, not both."

Rachel contorted her face. "I'm really confused now."

"Maybe if you told me a little more about this situation, I could figure it out."

"Oh, I don't think you want to be pulled in on this." Rachel issued a warning look. "This is what Matt wanted to put me on Haldol for."

"I remember your telling me that. What's the big deal?"

Rachel gave a hesitant look.

"Don't worry," MacKenzie assured her, "I can handle Matt."

"OK. I need to find out how a child Dr. Chan delivered could be AB if her mom is O."

"Chan? Why didn't you say he was involved to begin with?"

"Why does it matter?"

"Just that everyone knows he's big into in vitro fertilization; he probably implanted an embryo into this woman—what's her name?" MacKenzie read the fine print at the top of the page. "Prescott, hmmm."

"Yeah, but don't they usually use the sperm from the father and combine it with the mother's egg? If they did that, the blood types would match. Right?"

"Right."

"So how did he do it?"

"Can't answer you there. Why don't you just ask this woman directly?"

"She's in Chicago."

"So call her on the phone or write a letter. Seems simple to me."

"You don't understand. I tried before, but maybe a letter would be less threatening. . . ."

"Threatening? What's there to be threatened about?"

"If Elise—the child—is not really her daughter, maybe she fears she could lose her."

"That's an interesting theory, but it assumes the mother has a healthy attachment to the girl."

"What do you mean?"

"In order to be protective and worried about losing a daughter, that presumes a strong mother-child bond."

P r o g e n y

"So why wouldn't she have bonded?"

"It's been my experience that women who've become pregnant via IVF have a more difficult time developing attachments to their babies, especially if they've had to rely on egg and sperm donors."

"That makes no sense at all. Most women in that category have been trying for years to get pregnant. They desperately want a child."

"True. But what's the motivation? If it's just to produce a child to satisfy their own ego, then loving the child unconditionally becomes difficult—especially if the child doesn't fulfill their expectations. And if the child they end up bearing isn't really their child—genetically speaking—then all sorts of psychological factors come into play."

"Just because a child doesn't possess your genetic code doesn't mean you won't love the baby. Look at all the adoptive parents who have perfectly healthy relationships with their children."

"Rachel, adoptive parents fall into a completely different category. What we have here is not your normal parenting situation. The mind-set is completely different. Manipulating reproduction tends to encourage one to view children as products, as property. It colors the whole way we look at the meaning of having a child. Consider the pregnancy experience itself—there's got to be a tremendous amount of ambivalence over carrying a child other than your own. It's one thing to conceive your own flesh and blood, then slowly get used to the idea of having the baby and attaching before you even give birth."

Rachel nodded knowingly as she thought about Leah, her daughter, for that is what she and Matt had decided to name her. Her love and concern had grown during the pregnancy. Still, she was finding it difficult to produce mothering feelings spontaneously. Maybe MacKenzie was right; maybe mothering instincts didn't just happen overnight. Maybe it did take time.

MacKenzie continued, "Think about it; it's more difficult to bond if you really don't know who you're bonding with. Trust me; it isn't just my experience; the research bears this out. As far as this situation goes, what do you know about the family dynamics?"

"Very little, I suppose. I've just pieced together bits of information, and, well, I don't know if what you've said applies at all. I figure Mrs. Prescott is just older and more reserved in expressing affection and I—"

"Prescott. *Prescott*. That's why the name sounds so familiar."

"What?"

"I was discussing A.R.T.—assisted reproduction technologies—with a journalist the other night; and she asked me if I knew a Dr. Prescott from Chicago."

"You sure she said *Prescott*?"

"Positive."

"Well, I don't think it's related; it just couldn't be. There are lots of Prescotts in the Chicago area." Rachel remembered thumbing through the Downers Grove phone book. "It's probably different."

"Well, I find it all very interesting. Mind if I keep this for awhile? I'd like to share it with the journalist I mentioned." MacKenzie waved the lab report.

"For awhile, but eventually I'll need it back. Is this journalist named Helen by any chance?"

"Yes, why?"

"I think I met her in your waiting room."

"Could be. How did you get this lab profile in the first place?"

"Like I said before, I'm investigating a mother-daughter thing and, well, it's what Matt got up in arms about."

"What have you found out?"

"Can't tell you now. Give me a little more time. It doesn't make sense yet."

"Sounds suspicious."

"Well, like Matt would tell me, don't jump to conclusions. I may be assuming too much."

"Maybe so. But keep me posted anyway."

"Be glad to—when and if I find anything out."

"You're the reporter, if anyone can dig up answers, you're the one."

"Says you."

"Says me."

Lost in her own world, Rachel was fully absorbed in letter writing. MacKenzie had been called to attend a delivery, and Rachel was intent on expressing herself to the Prescotts in a nonthreatening manner when Matt's voice boomed across the room. "Whoa! Don't you look great today."

Caught off guard, Rachel quickly folded the letter and tucked it behind her. She peered into Matt's eyes, trying to tell if he had noticed.

"Oh, hi Darling. I thought you had a meeting."

"Canceled it." Matt smiled broadly, strolled over to the bed, and then leaned over and kissed her passionately on the lips. "So what are you up to?"

"Dr. MacKenzie came by, said I could go home soon . . . if I'm good."

"But can we trust you to be good?" He laughed knowingly. "I talked with her yesterday. She said you have to take it easy for awhile. Get your strength back before trying to do too much."

"I know. I know. She told me all that."

"So what are you hiding behind your back?" Matt was always too quick for her. He never missed a clue.

"Just a letter."

"To whom?"

"Oh Matt, I didn't want to go into it yet."

"Go into what?" Matt wasn't going to let up.

"It's a letter to Mrs. Prescott."

"*The* Mrs. Prescott? Rachel, are you crazy? They'll try to

put you away. You can't send that."

"I have to. I have to know the truth."

"Truth! What truth?" Matt was agitated. "It's time to move on, Rachel. We have a daughter to worry about. You can't keep hanging on to this Elise thing. Let it go."

He wasn't listening, not really. He ignored her statement about truth—almost as if he didn't want to know about her discovery—just plowed right past it with no intention of ever looking back. But Rachel wasn't intimidated by his tirade. She searched his eyes and softly but deliberately countered, "Matt, I found something out. Something not quite right."

"Rachel, please don't. . . ." Matt broke eye contact and turned away.

Distressed? Afraid? Rachel couldn't tell. "Darling, nothing's going to happen. They can't do anything to me. They can't hide the facts forever. Elise is not their daughter. She can't be."

Matt didn't respond to her comments, just held out his hand. "Give me the letter." He stood firm, waiting for Rachel to comply.

"Matt. Don't be so unreasonable. What's your problem?"

"MY PROBLEM! It's not my problem. You're the one with an overactive imagination!"

"Honey, don't get so upset. I'm not imagining anything. There are too many coincidences here. Dr. Chan was her doctor. He was my doctor. Elise's blood type and mine are the same. We even look alike. What more do you want?"

"I want you to let it go. I want to keep things just like they are—right now. Don't spoil what we have. I love you. I love our daughter. Please don't pursue this. Trust me. Just trust me on this. Let's go forward, leave the past behind. Can't you do that . . . for me?"

Rachel had never seen Matt like this. So persistent. So desperate. "OK." She reluctantly handed over the letter. "Are you happy now?"

Matt didn't reply, just silently read the letter, folded it over, and stuck it in his back pocket. There was no further discussion. "Come on," he finally said, "let's go see our daughter. She needs us."

Tug-
of-
War

Matt paced the floor in his office. The late afternoon sun was creeping into the room, casting ominous shadows, yet he refused to turn on the lights. Earlier he had left Rachel in the I.C.N. visiting Leah, saying he had a few patients to see. That was a lie. He had purposely cleared the entire day's schedule to spend time with his family. But now, all he wanted to do was hide.

P r o g e n y

After reading Rachel's letter to Mrs. Prescott, Matt had been unable to shake the nagging sensation that Rachel and Elise were somehow connected. What exactly was Chan's involvement, and what was Dr. Prescott afraid Rachel would discover? Perhaps Rachel really had stumbled onto something. But what? He pulled out the crumpled letter from his pocket, smoothed out the wrinkles and began rereading Rachel's letter to Mrs. Prescott:

> Dear Mrs. Prescott,
>
> I am writing to you as one mother to another. I know how much my visit upset you, and I'm sorry. I wasn't attempting to disrupt your life, but I needed to know the truth. If you were simply trying to protect your daughter, I understand. (I am finally a mother myself and have a daughter too. Her name is Leah.) I just want to understand the connection—and there is a connection! There is no way I could imagine this. Elise simply cannot be your biological daughter. Your blood type is different from hers (a lab report in your birth records verified this fact), and my obstetrician tells me it's genetically impossible for an O mother to have an AB child. Is it coincidental that my blood type is AB also? Is it coincidental that Dr. Chan was my doctor as well? Please understand my need to know the full story. Please tell me what you know about this—

A tug-of-war raged within. A part of Matt wanted answers to Rachel's questions—his questions, but the other part, fueled by guilt, stopped him cold. The message was loud and clear: *Bury the past; bury the past.* But his curiosity gained momentum, taunting him to search for the truth. Granted, it would have been easier to return to his denial mode, but somewhere inside, Matt knew that route was no longer an option. Something had to change. He couldn't continue to live with the guilt. He just couldn't.

Then the idea occurred to him: *I'll make amends. Surely, that will get rid of the guilt, and I can move on.* He stopped at his desk, flipped through his Rolodex, found a pager number, then pushed in the numbers on the phone. At least he was starting the process. At least he was doing something about his anguish, not just pacing the floor anymore. The phone rang once. Matt picked up the receiver. "Hello, Andy?"

"Matt? Is that you?"

"Yeah. I need to talk. Hope I didn't interrupt anything."

"No, no. I just couldn't figure out who was paging me at first. Didn't recognize the number. Almost didn't recognize your voice."

"Well, it's me all right."

"What's up?"

"Can you talk . . . now?"

"Sure, Matt. What's on your mind?"

"You know what we were discussing the other day about Chan?"

"Yeah."

"I want to help expose him. Let people know what he's doing."

"Why the sudden change of heart?"

"I've just been doing a lot of thinking."

"Sounds like there's more to it than that. Why now?"

"You know I used to work for Chan?"

"Right."

"Well, if I had known the whole story. . . ." Matt hesitated. He knew he wasn't being completely honest, so he added a disclaimer, "*Even if* I had known the whole story, it's hard to fathom. In my wildest dreams, I would've never believed he was capable of all this. It's unthinkable."

"Worse than unthinkable."

"How could it happen?"

"You know the old saying, 'All it takes for evil to triumph is for good men to do nothing.'"

"I can't keep silent any longer. What he's doing is wrong. Dead wrong. I want to stop him." The degree of contempt Matt felt rising within was surprising, if not frightening.

"You sure this isn't some sort of vendetta? Like maybe you've got a score to settle?"

Again Matt hesitated. But he knew he had to be truthful. No more deception. "Andy, it's a personal matter. Something in the past. It's not important now."

"Sure it is. Anything we can get on Chan, the better. Your testimony would mean a lot if you have specifics to share."

"Testimony?"

"For the senate subcommittee investigation. What do you think I've been talking about?"

"It's just that . . . I don't . . . I can't . . . It's personal. I can't go public with it."

"Matt, you said you wanted to help get Chan. You can't have it both ways. Either you spill the beans, or you don't. Simple as that."

"Don't push me, Andy. I have to think this through—decide what I can divulge. I don't want to hurt anyone."

"Hurt anyone? Matt, are you thinking clearly? Chan makes a business out of hurting people. He exploits women for money. You can't get much worse than that. If you have to hurt one person to stop him, don't you think it's worth it?"

"It's not that simple."

"Well, while you're figuring it out, I'm going to give Warren Still a call. He's head of the Family Protection Council on Capitol Hill. He'll have some suggestions I'm sure. Can I tell him to get in touch with you?"

"Sure."

"Thanks, Matt. I'll check back with you later."

"Right. Later." Matt returned the receiver to its cradle. His conversation with Rachel was replaying in his mind now. It was night when they had first visited the I.C.N. They had returned to Rachel's room and stayed up, deciding on Leah's name, talking and experiencing a special closeness. It had been one of those intimate moments that keep marriages going. Matt had wanted to come clean, to share everything about Chan, but was afraid. Even though a confession would have brought some relief, he knew the truth would hurt Rachel profoundly. Besides, there was a great probability that such a disclosure would shatter not only the intimacy of the moment but also their marriage as well. He closed that part of himself off, deciding to shield Rachel from such a harsh reality. Instead, he cupped her small, fragile hands in his and probed deep into her eyes. "Is there anything you couldn't forgive me for?"

Rachel replied lovingly and assuringly, "Of course not, Darling. I'll always love you. There's nothing you can do that could keep me from loving you. You know that."

Matt wasn't so sure.

Andy Macon and Matt found their seats and buckled in for the flight back to the Raleigh–Durham Airport. They had flown up to D.C. early that morning to meet with members of the congressional subcommittee and to attend a strategy meeting with Warren Still. Matt was mentally exhausted.

"I had no idea how organized the Family Protection Council is. Their arguments are impressive." Matt directed his comments to Andy even though the flight attendant had already begun her instructions.

"Yeah, I know. How'd you like the documentation they produced—especially the link between Chan and Dr. Forrest Prescott in Chicago?"

"Like I said, I was impressed. They really have their act together."

"You understand now why you have to go public with what you know? Why putting a face with the facts would make our case more convincing?"

"Yes. I just don't know if I'll be able to testify. . . . It's one thing to infiltrate Chan's organization in an attempt to gain access to information, but it's a whole different ball game to go public with a personal story."

"Matt, what's so difficult? What are you afraid of?"

"Something I did in the past . . . something I guess I'm ashamed of."

"It's the guilt, then, isn't it?"

"How'd you know?"

"Matt, everyone deals with guilt. You know that. You're a psychiatrist."

"Yeah, but this is different somehow. I can't seem to find a therapeutic outlet. Nothing works."

"Ah yes, getting rid of the guilt—a common problem. You know, Matt, this whole thing of helping us out in our fight against Chan, if it's some kind of penance you've worked up, let me tell you ahead of time, it won't work. The guilt will still be haunting you when the dust settles."

"So, you have any suggestions?" Matt looked earnestly at Macon.

"Of course I do. But do you really want to hear it?"

"At this point, I'll listen to anything."

"All right. Ever heard of the saying, 'And the truth shall set you free'?"

"From Gandhi?"

"No. Actually, straight from the lips of Christ. Know what truth he's referring to?"

"Not a clue."

"Well, you can't erase what you've done. Correct?"

"Correct."

"And you want to be free of the guilt. Right?"

"Right."

"Then you need someone to take the blame for you. Someone to 'set you free.'"

"That would work. Got any takers?"

"Actually, I do. The truth Christ is referring to in the passage I mentioned is how *he* atoned for guilt. How *he* took the penalty for your actions."

Matt took a deep breath and shook his head. "OK, Macon, I know where you're going with this, but it doesn't apply to me. You know I'm not a religious person."

"Face it, Matt. We're all hopelessly 'religious.' It's part of being human. We simply prefer creating our own gods so we can be in control; it makes it all a lot more manageable."

Matt was becoming increasingly uncomfortable. "Macon, just tell me how this has anything to do with me."

"Easy. There's a lawgiver, and he's written his laws on our hearts. When we transgress those laws, we experience a sense of remorse. That's where your guilty conscience comes from, and no amount of penance will take away the condemnation you feel."

"There's no need to bring God into this, Andy. Can't I just be sorry I did something wrong?"

"Wrong by whose standards?"

"Mine, I guess."

"But Matt, it isn't just wrong because you broke some self-imposed standard. You can't just explain away your guilt by saying you failed yourself. There's more at stake here."

Matt threw him a puzzled look.

"There are absolute standards, and from the sound of things, you violated them."

"I know; I know. I already admitted that."

"No, you only admitted that you broke *your* standards. I'm talking about God's standards."

"So? What's your point."

"If there were no moral absolutes, then you could just reset your own standards and eliminate God from the equation. You could tell yourself that in this particular case what you did was right . . . and necessary. No more guilt. Instant absolution." Macon looked Matt squarely in the eye, "But it doesn't work that way, does it?"

Matt thought for a moment. "OK, it doesn't work. Are you happy?" The conversation was starting to sound repetitious to Matt. He knew Andy could go on forever, and he didn't have the energy to argue. "I know you mean well Andy, but I'm really not interested in this, and now is just not a good time to deal with it. Can you get me *saved* some other time?" Matt was purposely distancing himself from Macon.

"Look, Matt," Macon's dander was up now, "this is not about making me happy. And for the record, I can't save anyone. And even if I could, what exactly would you be saved from?"

"Huh?" Matt was having difficulty focusing on the conversation.

"What would you be saved from? Discomfort from your guilt?"

"Oh, I don't know, Macon. What are you getting at?" Matt's eyelids were getting heavier by the moment, and he could barely keep them open.

Macon plunged ahead full force, continuing his diatribe undeterred. "The crux of the matter, that's what. You'd be saved from cosmic justice."

"Cosmic justice?" The last comment jogged Matt's attention. "You mean like 'an eye for an eye'?" He couldn't contain himself and laughed out loud. "Macon, you crack me up. Where do you get this stuff?"

"Stuff? It's not 'stuff,'" Macon said angrily." Listen, when you find a way to atone for your own sins, let me know."

"Look, I don't have a death wish if that's what you mean, and I'm really tired." Matt yawned. "Can we talk about this some other time?"

"Sure. But you do understand the doctrine of substitutionary atonement, don't you? Matt? Matt. . . ?"

Matt had drifted off to sleep.

CHAPTER 15

Alliance

Early summer mornings on the deck overlooking Rachel's herb garden offered a peaceful beginning to Matt's usual, hectic schedule of juggling rounds on in-house patients, outpatient clinic visits with residents, and med student teaching responsibilities. Rachel and Matt had made a ritual of stealing time together over coffee before going their separate ways. Often it was the only time when they were both coherent.

"Mmmm." Matt sank back into his chair, savoring his first swallow of coffee. "So, how'd you sleep last night? When I came home, you were out."

"I tried to wait up, but I was exhausted . . . dreamed something a little unsettling though. I was gonna tell you about it, but now I can't even remember. It's all a blur."

"About Leah?"

"Oh, I don't know. I just carried away an empty feeling."

"Well, don't concentrate on your dreams. Concentrate on reality." He leaned over and tried to read the title of the booklet she was flipping through. "What's that?"

"Infant stimulation protocols from the University of Virginia at Charlottesville."

"Where'd you get that?"

"Went over to The Frank Porter Graham Developmental Center and asked if they had anything on stimulating preemies."

"Didn't the nurses give you enough info already?"

"Yeah, but nothing in-depth. I wanted the hows and whys. This details the research that's been done. Do you realize just stroking babies helps promote brain development?"

"I'm not surprised."

"And now I understand why they cover their little eyes at intervals. It's important to maintain wake and sleep rhythms."

"I'm glad you're keeping busy. I wish I could spend

more time in the nursery with you and Leah."

"Don't feel guilty. I've explained your schedule to Leah. We both understand."

"Well, it's nice to know both my girls are in agreement. Give her a kiss for me. I'll drop by the nursery later, when I get a spare moment." Matt stood up and gave Rachel a long, solid good-bye kiss. "There, that should hold you until I get back." He smiled suggestively.

As if to protect herself from his advances, Rachel tautly pulled her robe across her chest, then rendered the deepest, Southern drawl possible. "My, my. You doctors are all alike. Only after one thang. . ." She batted her eyelashes as she fanned herself with a pretend fan.

"And you love it." Matt spoke authoritatively but gently, grabbing her for one last kiss. Then he vaulted down the wooden stairs and headed around the corner of the house towards the driveway.

Matt joined the psych residents and hurried through rounds, trying desperately to maintain his focus on the hospitalized patients. Today was the day Warren Still had arranged for Matt to meet with a reporter named Helen Bohannon. She was the one who was supposed to have answers to his questions about Chan and the Chinese connection. Matt's instructions were to meet an Asian woman at

1:00 P.M. at Four Eleven West, an Italian restaurant on Franklin Street. She would be wearing a green jacket.

The morning flew by as Matt responded to one crisis after another. The administrative headaches only added to his anxiety level. Finally, at 12:45, he broke away, leaving instructions with the chief resident. Knowing he didn't have time to walk across campus, he headed out to the doctor's parking lot, hating the thought of driving over in a vehicle heated up by the morning sun. Although he had spent the last weekend replacing the compressor for the air conditioner, it didn't compensate for the car's ovenlike temperature. The cool air didn't even kick in until he drove into the parking lot beside Four Eleven West.

Matt parked and fed the meter several quarters, then hastened toward the entrance. A rush of cold air hit him as he opened the restaurant door, when he caught a whiff of fresh, baked bread and immediately remembered why he liked this place so much. The hostess looked up with a warm smile. "One?"

"No, two. I'm meeting someone. Helen Bohannon."

"Oh, yes. She's waiting. Follow me."

The hostess led him through an archway to a table in the brick-walled atrium. A tall, slender woman stood, extending her hand for Matt to shake. Her green eyes matched the brocade jacket she wore, and her dark hair was styled smartly around her face. "Dr. Hamilton, I'm Helen Bohannon. So nice to meet you."

"Same here." Matt shook her hand—noting her manicured nails—and figured she was around thirty-five. Then they both sat down. "So, how long have you been waiting?" Matt asked, eyeing her half-empty glass of tea.

"Oh, not long, about 30 minutes."

Matt quickly issued an apology. "Sorry. I thought Warren said 1:00."

"He did. But my plane got in earlier than expected, and this place was so easy to find. I thought it would take longer. No problem."

Matt relaxed somewhat, "You flew in from Chicago?"

"Yes—I was following up on some research—it was a direct flight, not bad at all. Just glad to get back. I love this section of the country."

"It is nice. We really like it here."

"We?"

"My wife. She's a journalist too, well . . . was. . . . She's a mother right now."

"Good for you . . . I mean for both of you. How many children do you have?"

Matt shot a pained look and answered tentatively, "One, a daughter, born prematurely. She's still in intensive care."

"I'm sorry. Well, I shouldn't be prying anyway."

"It's OK. It's common knowledge. It's just so uncertain right now."

"Be thankful you can have children. I can't. My husband and I've finally accepted the fact that we'll have to adopt."

"That's tough."

"Yeah, it's been a hard thing to accept."

"Well, there's in vitro fertilization and lots of new technologies that—"

"I know all that. It's more complicated. Believe me, I've exhausted all my options."

The waitress interrupted their conversation. "Ready to order?"

"Sure," Matt broke in, motioning towards Helen. "This lady's been waiting long enough. Bring us two orders of your Chicken Marsala with fettuccini—"

"Excuse me," Helen sat straight up, cutting Matt off. "You may want the Chicken Marsala, but I've been sitting here memorizing the menu, and I'd like pasta primavera." Her tone was definitive as she turned toward the waitress and handed the menu back.

The waitress dutifully scribbled down the orders, then looked questioningly at Matt, "And what for you to drink?"

"Tea," Matt answered sheepishly.

"Alrighty then, be right back." The waitress smiled and left.

"So," Matt shifted in his seat, refocusing on Helen's previous comments. "Does your infertility have something to do with why you're out to get Chan?"

"In a way, I suppose. It's what got me started. I began tracking Chan after researching his methods. It all seemed promising at first."

"Well, that answers one of my questions."

"Oh?" Helen looked puzzled.

"I was suspicious of your motives. Wondered what a reputable reporter was doing chasing down Chan. It just didn't compute. Most people don't have a problem with Chan. He's very well respected."

"I'm aware of that. But those people don't really know about him. They couldn't. I mean, if they did, they'd be appalled."

"That's not the impression I get. Lots of people know exactly what he's about and don't think twice."

"Exactly. They don't think. They don't ask questions; they don't wonder where he gets the aborted tissue. All that matters to them is that 'the end justifies the means.'" Her voice was rising in intensity as she continued. "That's how they can ignore taking aborted tissue for research in the first place. It's like the Nazi doctors saying, 'If you're going to kill all these people, at least take the brains so we can use them.'"

"You're pretty worked up over this, aren't you?"

"Can you blame me?" Helen asked defensively.

"Well—your points are valid, and your reasoning is convincing—to a point. I just can't get over how much you sound like a friend of mine."

"What are you talking about?"

"My friend—he's got pretty strong religious convictions."

"What's that got to do with me? You don't have to be religious to see how unethical Chan is."

"That's not what my friend would say. He'd say that unless you begin with God your motives don't have a starting point. Coming up with an ethical conclusion would be inconsistent. He says most ethical people borrow their conclusions from the Judeo-Christian ethic."

"Hadn't thought of it that way. Is that what you believe?" Her stare was unavoidable.

"Not there yet. Just beginning to look at my assumptions." Matt pushed away from the table, obviously uncomfortable with Helen's line of questioning.

The waitress reappeared with Matt's tea and two steaming bowls of pasta.

"Well," Helen proceeded, swirling vermicelli around her fork, "I got pulled into the ethics debate by a lawyer friend of mine. She raised a lot of issues I'd never even considered." Helen looked up at Matt questioningly, "Did you know that only a few states prohibit using fetal tissue in transplantation? And the laws against abortion for profit aren't enforced, so a woman could get pregnant just to sell her baby for parts! I mean, who's going to stop her? Then there's the issue of consent. According to my friend, a fetus should be treated like a child for custody purposes with both parents consenting to abortion and the donation of fetal tissue. But do you think that happens?"

Helen didn't give him a chance to respond but took a deep breath and pressed on, "Not a chance. You won't find anyone signing consent forms under those conditions. But, if there was an automobile accident and someone wanted an organ for transplantation, you better believe they'd have someone signing on the dotted line—even if the family was deeply grieving, even if it was the middle of the night. Strictly policy, you know. Sounds a bit like a double standard to me, an ethical nightmare—"

Matt broke in. He was starting to wonder if Helen's passion was obscuring her objectivity. "How does all this relate to Chan?"

"How about harvesting aborted fetal ovaries and transplanting them in—"

Again, Matt interrupted her. "Harvesting fetal ovaries? That wouldn't be a simple matter. Keeping the tissue alive is a major problem, not to mention the immaturity of the ovaries. I'm sure it's a little more involved than you make it sound."

"OK, so I don't know all the medical lingo to explain how it's done, but I do know Chan's been successfully transplanting fetal ovaries in mice."

"Well, if he can make it work in humans, wouldn't that solve your infertility problem? What's your hang-up?"

"First off, the legal end is questionable, and even if it were legal, it's unconscionable to think of having a murdered baby's ovaries inside your body. Then, what if you did conceive, whose baby would it really be? And what would you tell the children? 'There's no record, no information about your biological mother. She was an aborted fetus.'" Helen sighed, exasperated by the whole scenario. "Enough of my tirade. What else can I tell you about Chan?"

Matt, anxious to get on with the interview and off the ethics issue, leaned forward. "Basics. Tell me what you know about Biotech."

"The quick and easy answer—a front for a very lucrative abortion business. They run clinics all across the country."

"But what about the Chinese connection? I know Chan exports fetal tissue, but why? The Chinese should have plenty of their own from all the forced abortions."

"It's my understanding that Chan has ongoing collaborative research with the Chinese. I'm not sure who initiated it, but Chan began shipping fetal tissue over to them in the late '70s. He could guarantee fresh, uncontaminated specimens because of the particular abortion procedure he had developed, and that was important to them. Conditions in hospitals and clinics in China are extremely backward. You might as well be in a Third World country."

"How do you know all of this?"

"I spent some time in Hong Kong when I served as a foreign correspondent—toured facilities on the mainland. Things haven't changed much since then, and I still have my contacts."

"OK. So what you're saying is that the abortion procedure he developed keeps the tissue intact and alive long enough to put it on ice and ship it. So his Chinese partners are actually using U.S. fetal tissue in medical experiments?"

"For specific projects. I'm sure they use their own

supply for regular medicinal purposes. According to tradition, they believe human fetuses have healing properties. You do know that?"

"I've heard that. But I'm still unclear. Why China?"

"Why anywhere? Money. Big bucks. And besides, you don't have to worry about the legalities in China. Remember, the ban on fetal tissue research was only recently lifted in the U.S."

"Well, it doesn't matter if it was lifted, Americans won't tolerate experiments on aborted fetuses. There's something inherently wrong with that."

"You'd think that would be the case—opposition to using fetal tissue for cosmetics and such—but don't count on it. Like I said earlier, people don't seem to care. As long as they can benefit in some way, they just look the other way."

"Cosmetics?"

"Sure. It's widely rumored that cosmetic companies use fetal brain cells, livers, and kidneys to produce 'rejuvenation' treatments."

"In America?"

"Like I said, rumored in the U.S., but for sure in France. Face it, it doesn't matter where it's done, Americans just import it. They couldn't care less how they got it."

"But why? Why would Chan be a part of an operation that exploits women?"

"I don't know. Maybe his mother abandoned him when he was a little boy or something. But just listen to him sometime; you can almost hear the disdain for women in his voice." Her voice trailed off as she reflected on her premise. Suddenly she blurted out, "Maybe it's a power thing."

Matt didn't respond. He was staring down into his bowl of pasta, deep in thought.

"Hey," Helen raised her voice, trying to pull Matt back into the conversation. "You're the psychiatrist; you figure it out."

"It's hard to accept." Matt slowly looked up, shaking his head. "I used to think Chan wanted to help women. I idolized him. He was my mentor. I would've done anything he asked—without question." Matt stopped abruptly, realizing the implications of what he had said.

"You're not alone. He's deceived a lot of people."

"Well, that's no excuse. I know that now."

"Warren said something about you needing to come to terms with your past if you were going to testify for us."

"Right. I've been trying to deal with that, but it's not easy. It's easier just to leave the past behind."

"Is that what you want to do?"

"I'm not sure. But for now, let's stick with the present, concentrate on getting evidence against Chan—like Warren suggested."

"Well, you're definitely the one for the job. Chan won't suspect a thing if you infiltrate his setup. If it were me, now, that would be a different story."

"How so?"

"He'd recognize me."

"You sound pretty sure of that."

"I ought to be. I challenged him at an N.I.H. ceremony once—asked him a few pointed questions."

"What did he say?"

"Didn't say much of anything, just had security cart me out."

"I guess he would remember something like that."

"I guess so. If not, there's the time I covered a protest outside his lab. The look he gave me that day—well, let's just say if looks could kill, I'd be dead. I'm sure he—" Helen gasped, freezing in place. "Don't turn around," she spoke in hushed tones. "There's a man seated a few tables back who was in the lobby yesterday as I left my friend's law office."

"Problem?"

"It strikes me as strange. What are the odds that that man would be eating lunch in the same place as me—in Chapel Hill? I've often sensed someone watching me but never had anything tangible to go on. Until now."

"Why would someone be following you?"

"I don't know. Maybe Chan's worried. From what I know about him and his associates, I wouldn't doubt it at all."

"What about his associates?"

"As far as I'm concerned, they're thugs. Would have no qualms about doing whatever it takes to achieve their ends."

"You can't be serious. You make it sound like they're criminals."

"I'm beginning to think they are. I've heard stories

about suspicious accidents happening to people who were too vocal."

"Accidents?"

"Yeah, like brakes mysteriously going out."

"Hmm. . . . My wife had an accident—ran a traffic light. We just assumed she went into labor." Matt mused a moment, shaking his head as he thought. "Surely, there's no connection."

"I know I sound paranoid, but can we talk somewhere else? I'd feel a lot more comfortable." Helen was insistent.

"Sure." Matt pushed back an empty dish of pasta and stood up. "Follow me."

CHAPTER 16

The
Mission

Faces were becoming more familiar and the atmosphere less threatening at the I.C.N. A month had passed, and Rachel now knew all the names of Leah's nurses and when to expect their shifts to start. Sharon was her favorite, a perky little blonde who cared deeply for the small charges assigned to her care. Today, Sharon gave Rachel an "all is not well" look as she entered the unit.

"What's the problem?" Rachel quizzed, trusting Sharon's assessment of Leah's condition.

"Beginning signs of N.E.C."

Rachel raised her eyebrows. "I thought I'd heard all the names you guys throw out, but I'm clueless on this one."

"Necrotizing entercolitis—it's an intestinal disorder. Sort of an infection. You know how we always measure Leah's tummy?"

Rachel nodded affirmatively.

"If it gets too big, we know she's not absorbing her feedings, then we suspect N.E.C."

"How can you know for sure?"

"Take an X-ray."

"Have they taken one? Is it serious? Is she gonna be alright?" The questions spewed out.

"The doctor ordered an X-ray, but it may be nothing. No need to get upset until we know something for sure."

"What happens if she has it?"

"Ultimately, surgery. But that's a ways off. Like I said, don't worry until there's something to worry about."

That's easy for you to say. It's my baby! Rachel didn't dare speak her thoughts out loud; Sharon would be offended. All the nurses worked tirelessly around the clock caring for these babies. But it was still different, Rachel reminded herself. Leah was her child, the child she planned to take home. And neither she nor Leah needed a setback like this.

Not knowing was always the most difficult thing. And

waiting. A gnawing, restless feeling crept in, and Rachel attempted to escape its reach by wandering away from Leah's side. She walked around the unit and then crossed into the intermediate care area, where babies moved when they graduated from intensive care. Every mother envisioned her baby ending up over there. All other thinking was taboo.

Rachel thought about the powerful maternal feelings she had developed for Leah. It was a good sign. Her Elise obsession had all but disappeared; Leah was now her primary concern. *Maybe that's the way it is supposed to be,* she thought. *Maybe Matt was right. Maybe she read too much into a connection between herself and Elise. Just because Elise had the same blood type didn't mean they were related, and to tell Elise that her mother wasn't really her biological mother would be cruel. Devastating actually. What good would come of telling her? She should leave it alone and concentrate on Leah. That was the right thing to do.*

In the far corner of the intermediate nursery, Rachel noticed a mother cradling a baby wrapped in a blanket. Slowly rocking back and forth, the woman was completely absorbed in her child. The picture haunted Rachel. Her baby wasn't even connected to anything—no wires, no tubes. There was something peculiar about it. She could sense it.

As she drew closer, she noticed that the infant the woman clutched possessively was cloaked by the blanket and barely visible. Rachel approached the pair cautiously and spoke tentatively. "Hi."

There was no response. Trying again, she raised her

voice. "Hi. I'm Rachel. My baby's on the other side." Rachel pointed to the area beyond the glass partition. The woman rocking her baby didn't seem interested in making friends, but Rachel gave it one last shot anyway. "I'm waiting for them to do X-rays."

The woman wearily lifted her head. Her eyes were swollen and the dark circles, pronounced. "I guess you don't know," she said in a tired voice.

"Know what?"

"My baby's dying. No one talks about it. They just leave me to myself."

"I'm sorry. I didn't . . . didn't know." Rachel stumbled over her words. Was she intruding, invading a mother's privacy?

"No harm done."

Even though turning and leaving would dispel the awkwardness, Rachel felt compelled to stay. In fact, she had to stay. Ever since noticing this woman, Rachel had been strangely drawn to her. Continuing the conversation was inevitable.

"Would you like to talk about it?"

"There's nothing to talk about. Didn't you hear me? My baby's dying."

"Yes, I heard you. I'm just concerned. I know how it is to lose a child. I know how bad it hurts."

The woman looked straight into Rachel's face and said bitterly, "You know how it is to have a defective child? A child no one wants to hold? A child that's just a case for the

204

medical books? Are you wanting to get a look too so you can say you've seen a baby with no skull or brain?"

"No. NO! You've got it wrong. I had no idea." Rachel was stunned but more determined than ever to reach out. "Are you saying your baby is . . ."

"Anencephalic." The woman finished Rachel's sentence. "Doctors say he only has a brain stem. That's what keeps him breathing. Soon enough his little heart will just stop. Can't do anything but wait."

"Is this your only child?"

"Yes. My one and only, and I'm not about to shorten his life one iota. I don't care what they say."

"What do you mean shorten his life?"

"They want me to give him over for some kind of organ program. Want his organs before he dies. Ain't no way I'm gonna do that."

"Who wants you to do that?"

"Doctors, nurses. All of 'em. But I ain't playing along. No sir. You can't convince me either. Just wasting your breath."

"Please slow down. I'm not a doctor or a nurse. I just have a baby in here. Who wants your baby's organs?"

"Some research people. Come by to talk. Acted all sweet. Then they hit me with it. Wanted me to sign some papers, but I wouldn't do it. Nurses said I should." She was shaking her head disapprovingly. "Nope. Like I said, no way I'm gonna do that. Let my baby die in peace. God decides when to take him. I'm not rushing it."

Rachel felt like she had been hit broadside by a tractor trailer. The emotional impact of what this lady had shared was staggering. The desire to help intensified.

"Mrs.? I'm sorry I don't know your name."

"Wilson. Brenda Wilson."

"Brenda, is it OK to call you that?"

"Sure."

"Do you have family to help you? A husband?"

"A husband. But he left me when the baby was born. Couldn't handle it."

"I'm so sorry. I wish there was something I could do to help. Is there anything?"

"Don't think so . . . I'm just tired, so very tired." The woman slumped down and resumed rocking.

Rachel put her hand on Brenda's arm and gently squeezed. "I really am sorry, and I'm here if you need to talk."

The woman looked up again, and Rachel saw a tear streaming down her cheek. Her cold, hard exterior was beginning to melt. "I just want to do the right thing. Don't want to be selfish. Am I? They said his death could help others live. I'm so confused." She hung her head and wept quietly.

Rachel's anger flared. How could someone be so insensitive? Pressuring this poor woman at a vulnerable time in her life and trying to make her feel guilty. It was simply unacceptable. "Who told you these things?"

"A guy, said he represented a group that wanted to help

others. Gave me his card. Said to call if I changed my mind."
She reached into her pocket and pulled out a business card.
"You take it. I don't reckon I'll be needing it."

Although the card held no meaning for Rachel, she
took it anyway. Maybe Matt would know something. At least
he'd know how to stop this kind of harassment. And surely,
he'd know the ethical standards established for this type of
situation. Rachel turned the card over in her hand and read
the inscription:

Douglas Kao, Research Assistant
Biotechnology International
Research Triangle Park, N.C.
919-345-9782

"Listen. I'm going to ask my husband about this. They
can't force you to do anything. You have every right to let
your baby die peacefully." The woman had withdrawn again,
rocking her baby and humming what sounded like a lullaby.
It was a private moment and Rachel felt like an intruder.
She slowly backed away and whispered, "I'll come back
later."

The name 'Biotech' troubled Rachel as she returned to
Leah's side. Wasn't that the name of Dr. Prescott's research
company? But how could that be? The Biotech this woman
talked about was in Research Triangle Park; Prescott was in
Chicago. . . .

P r o g e n y

Rachel hated waiting. Waiting for the doctor to read Leah's X-rays, waiting to ask Matt her questions. On one hand, she wanted to slip right over to Matt's office. On the other hand, she couldn't bear to leave Leah until the verdict was in about N.E.C. So why couldn't she just leave the I.C.N. and come right back? What was holding her there? She knew the answer. It was another sign that she had bonded with her daughter. Feeling protective was right and good.

But choosing between Matt and Leah was a new experience, a juggling act to which she must adjust. She chastised herself for being so consumed with Leah that she had neglected Matt. She hoped he hadn't noticed, and maybe he hadn't. He was spending a lot of time with Andy Macon lately, more so than usual. Although she wasn't exactly sure what they were working on, most probably, it involved the ethics report.

"Mrs. Hamilton?" Dr. Saldana's greeting startled Rachel as he approached Leah's isolette.

"Oh, hi." Rachel responded, looking up from the stool she was seated on. "Have you gotten the results from the X-rays yet?"

"Just now. Good news to report—Leah isn't in any immediate danger. I didn't see any bubbles in the intestines, so I think we're OK for now. But just in case, I'm putting her N.P.O.—that means no feedings—for about 14 days and starting her on a course of antibiotics. We don't want to take any chances with this. Any questions?"

"What a relief." Rachel sighed as the tension drained from her body. Then she verbalized the fear she had been battling since first hearing about the possibility of an infection. "I thought N.E.C. meant surgery."

"That's the worst case scenario. Prevention is the key, and if we watch her carefully, we can catch it before it gets out of control."

"But I thought my breast milk was supposed to protect her from things like this. Are you telling me that all that pumping is for naught?"

"Certainly not. Don't second-guess what you've been doing. Breast milk is the best preventative measure we have. Just give it a little time. We'll resume her feedings as soon as we think she can tolerate it. Just keep pumping, and we can freeze the milk until she's ready. Here's some information about N.E.C. It'll help explain things more fully. Any other questions?"

"No. Thank you." Rachel took the handout he offered and smiled weakly as he turned and left. She didn't know enough to ask intelligent questions, and she wasn't about to ask something that sounded as ignorant as she felt. She glanced down at the information and began reading:

YOUR BABY HAS N.E.C.

Necrotizing entercolitis (NEC) is a problem for 5 percent of newborn infants. For reasons not clearly understood, the delicate lining of the intestines is damaged, predisposing the baby to infection in that area.

What causes NEC? Oxygen is vital to sustain life. Any time a part of the body is deprived of oxygen, it will be damaged. A good example of this concept is a heart attack. During a heart attack blood flow to the heart is reduced, thereby causing damage to that particular muscle.

Babies receiving an inadequate supply of oxygen during a difficult delivery, or because of heart or respiratory problems, often develop N.E.C. This is a result of insufficient oxygen reaching the intestines. The body will always try to protect "vital" organs, such as the heart and brain. Thus, if there is not enough oxygen to go around, the available oxygen is shunted away from the intestines to "save" more important areas. Unfortunately, this protective function may leave a portion of the intestines damaged. Once damaged, there is a greater chance of developing an infection.

Premature infants seem most vulnerable to N.E.C. not only because of their fragile intestines and the likelihood of developing respiratory distress but also because they are deficient in immunities against bacteria. They simply do not have the factors necessary to fight off germs. Sometimes, the body's otherwise "normal" bacteria will invade the damaged area, creating further problems. Sometimes the damage is even extensive enough to warrant surgery.

Can N.E.C. be prevented? Yes and no. Since situations which reduce blood flow to the intestines can't always be prevented, it is more productive to focus on ways to decrease the chance of infection. This means strictly following the ritual of careful hand-washing. In addition, since breast milk offers protective properties specific to the baby's digestive tract, all babies would benefit from receiving their mother's freshly expressed milk. Finally, closely observing the baby for sudden changes in behavior and appearance can reveal early signs of N.E.C. Treated early, N.E.C. is less of a problem. The infant who doesn't "look good," begins to feed poorly, has trouble keeping warm, or starts having apena/bradycardia and becomes less responsive to stimuli is suspect.

How is N.E.C. treated?

Once a baby is suspected of having N.E.C., frequent evaluations are done, including laboratory tests and X-rays. If X-rays confirm the presence of N.E.C., oral feedings are discontinued. The baby usually remains N.P.O. (nothing by mouth) for about two weeks, enabling the intestines to heal. During this time antibiotics are given to help fight the infections.

As with all problems a baby encounters while hospitalized, it is the parents who must live through the day-to-day stress of uncertainty. While the cycle of hope and fear may seem unending, it is important for parents to continue supporting their baby by holding, rocking, and talking. Equally important is making sure a pacifier is available to meet sucking needs during the time a baby is NPO. Medical treatment is essential, but nothing can ever replace a parent's involvement.

The instant Rachel finished reading, her mind started churning out thoughts: *Hmmm. Parental involvement? Just where is Matt? Where is your father, Leah?*

Normally, Matt would have stopped by the unit by now. Rachel suddenly felt alone. It didn't take much prompting for the old feelings to resurface, and although Matt was usually part of the picture, his absence now produced an ache that was all too familiar.

Rachel leaned over toward Leah, opened the isolette door, placed her hand through the porthole and delicately stroked her daughter's head. "I'm going to find your father," she whispered. "Be back real soon. Love you."

The nurse, standing within earshot, smiled understandingly as Rachel carefully closed the isolette door and gathered up her belongings. "See you in a bit," Rachel nodded to the nurse and proceeded out of the unit.

Preoccupied with thoughts of Leah's vacillating condition, as well as thoughts of the woman and her dying baby, Rachel didn't notice Dr. MacKenzie standing in the entrance to the I.C.N.

"Hello, stranger." A familiar voice called out.

Rachel looked up. "Oh! What are you doing down here?"

"Checking on a baby I delivered last night. How are you?"

"Fine. Same old, same old."

"Have time for a cup of coffee?"

"That would be nice, but I need to touch base with Matt first. Can we meet in about thirty minutes?"

MacKenzie glanced at her watch. "I think that can be arranged. Coffee shop?"

"Sure. See you then." Rachel twirled around and quickened her pace as she headed toward Matt's office.

The long walk over to the psych wing exhausted Rachel. She had not fully regained her strength since her discharge from the hospital, and the combination of staying in bed for all those months of pregnancy plus the added stress of the accident and C-section had weakened her considerably. The energy it took to hike over to Matt's office surprised her. By the time she got to the reception area, she was out of breath and physically depleted. She grabbed the first chair in sight and collapsed.

The receptionist heeded Rachel's arrival and spoke up, anticipating her question. "You just missed him. He left here in a huff."

"You mean he was upset?"

"Seemed so to me. He sure didn't like my asking questions about where he was going. Shot me a 'none of your business look.' Good thing he didn't have any more patients to see today. Wouldn't want them to have to talk with an ornery doc."

"You think he might've written where he was going on his calendar?"

"You can look. I wasn't gonna snoop myself, but you're welcome to. After all, you *are* his wife. It's probably on his desk."

Rachel picked herself up and sauntered by the front desk as the receptionist rattled on. She wandered down the hallway to Matt's office, curious to discover his whereabouts. Sure enough, his calendar was lying open on his desk, and the notation leaped out at her: 4:30, Chan, Research Triangle Park.

Why in the world was Matt going to see Chan? Scanning the open page for further clues, Rachel found a telephone number Matt had jotted down alongside the appointment time. Without thinking, she picked up the phone and called the number.

"Hello. You have reached Biotechnology Research International. If you have the extension of the person you are calling, press one now. If you would like to speak with an operator, press 2 now."

The recorded message sent a shock wave through her body. *BIOTECH. Chan's with Biotech?* Rachel remembered Dr. MacKenzie's remarks about Chan's unorthodox positions. She pulled out the business card the woman in the I.C.N. had given her. Did Matt know about Chan and this connection with Biotech? And what about Chan's connection to Elise—afterall, he was the doctor who delivered her. Rachel had to know. No more unanswered questions. She hung up the phone and decided to follow Matt. It was an impulsive decision yet imperative, nevertheless. Her mission was clear-cut.

Traffic slowed her down. But it really didn't matter; Rachel had no idea where she was going. The research park

215

area was unfamiliar to her, forcing her to drive around until she spotted a sign for Biotech. The digital clock in the car registered 5:00 P.M. as she approached a huge brick complex studded with windows. A prominately displayed sign reading Biotechnologies Research International revealed that her destination was at hand. She turned into the parking lot, where a string of cars lined up to exit. *It's closing time; everyone's leaving.*

Two main entrances, one for a clinic, the other marked Research Facilities competed for selection. She chose the latter, parked and hurried inside, hoping to find a directory. Conveniently, a listing of offices, including Chan's, was mounted on the wall beside the elevators. *Executive suite no less,* Rachel mused as she read over the listing of names while waiting for the elevator. When the doors finally opened, a crowd emptied out, and she stepped aboard, riding all the way to the top.

A panoramic view greeted Rachel as the doors opened on the fifth floor. The offices and reception areas were deserted, and all was quiet, except for some distant voices. *Matt has to be here somewhere.* She followed the voices to the end of the hall. The closer she got the more distinct the voices became, and at one point she recognized Matt's voice emanating from an open doorway. Although the lights in this outer office area were turned off, the inner office lighting cast a glow all the way into the hallway. She cautiously entered the outer office, drawing closer to the voices. The door to the

216

inner office—Chan's private suite—was open, allowing Rachel to hear clearly Chan's condescending lecture.

"Matt, we aren't foolish enough to fall for your scheme. We've been watching you and your wife for some time. I am well aware of your plans, so let me tell you up front: It won't work. Besides, I'm prepared to offer you a deal."

"I know about your deals. I'm not interested."

"But Matt. It's to protect your wife."

"Is that a threat?"

"Why, Matt, I'm surprised you would think such a thing." Chan's sarcasm was venomous. "I'm just concerned about Rachel's well-being, as you are. Correct me if I'm wrong, but she would be devastated if she knew the truth about our previous arrangement. Right?"

"You know she would be." Chan's intent was predictable. Matt braced himself for the inevitable deal.

"Let's just say," Chan continued, "if you agree to cooperate with us, we'll keep this little secret to ourselves."

How could Chan still have this kind of power over me? I can't let him do this. Matt mentally struggled to resist, refusing to fall prey again.

"It's over, Chan. I'll have no part in your business deals. Rachel is my concern, not yours. Stay out of our lives."

"Oh, so you want me to stay out of your lives now? That's not how you wanted it fifteen years ago. Seems to me, you gladly accepted my help then. Plan on telling Rachel how you sold your child to me? Blood money, I believe they call it?

Think she'll embrace you after hearing how you willingly consented to aborting the child without her knowledge?"

"You manipulated me."

"Now, now, Matt. You're a psychiatrist. Do you think I'll allow you to displace the blame onto me? You are responsible for your own actions—not me."

"How could you tell her? How can you be so heartless?" Matt blurted out his thoughts, knowing all the while that appealing to Chan's conscience was futile. A man like Chan had no conscience.

"Business is business," Chan replied callously. "All I ask is that you drop plans to testify against Biotech. I'll trade your silence for my silence. An easy proposition to accept."

"Listen, Chan. I've made my position clear: No deal. I've had enough of this deception. I'll tell Rachel myself." Matt didn't give himself time to think about the impact his confession would make. He just knew he couldn't give in to Chan, not now, not ever. "Face it Chan, even if I don't testify, someone else will nail you."

"Since when did you become the purist? You and your ethics committee are preparing to rubber-stamp physician-assisted suicide, and you point the finger at me? What a hypocrite."

"Hold on. I've been rethinking my stand."

"Give it up, Matt. You'll have a hard time convincing me or anyone else. Your track record is clear."

"Since when did my record become the issue here? As

far as I'm concerned, you're the issue, and what you're doing is flat out wrong."

"Where did this self-righteous act come from? You, of all people, know that everything at Biotech is strictly legal. And you won't find any evidence to the contrary."

"It doesn't matter if it's legal or not. It's unethical. You're marketing fetal tissue on the black market, and that's worse than unethical; it's barbaric."

"Matt, Matt, Matt." Chan shook his head. "There's no need for a black market. Research collaboration among professionals is expected. And as far as ethical violations, I suppose you have documentation to support your allegations?"

"I'll get it. . . ." Matt's voice trailed off. He knew he was there to get proof, and he had failed. His only hope now was to bluff Chan into revealing incriminating evidence. But what? The words came in a flash: "There's Elise Prescott. Pretty strong case of an ethical infraction there." Matt had no idea where his comment would lead but knew it was worth a try.

Chan was visibly shaken, but only for a moment. "Ah, yes. Elise. Beautiful girl. What was it that concerned you?"

"Same blood type as Rachel and clearly not Prescott's offspring."

"You do have a vivid imagination. Following in your wife's footsteps, I see."

"Knock off the charade. Genetic testing would be quite revealing . . . and conclusive."

Chan scoffed. "So I did a little experiment with the fetal ovaries I salvaged from the abortion and implanted an embryo into Mrs. Prescott. Nothing wrong with that. Solved her infertility problem, and I was a hero. No one objects to progress, Matt. You go public with this, and all you'll do is hurt the people you love. Is that what you want?"

Matt steadied himself. Chan's candid admission had dazed him. He took a deep breath and recovered his composure, intent on countering Chan. "The truth is what I want, and . . . the truth will set me free." Matt blurted the last part out unexpectedly.

"Aren't we the philosopher all of a sudden," Chan sneered, resuming his ruthless demeanor. "Matt, are you prepared for the world to know you sold your offspring for experimentation?"

"I had no idea . . . no knowledge of your plans."

"It doesn't matter what you knew back then. What matters is what the public will think of their impeccable Dr. Hamilton now. Trust me. You try to make me the bad guy, and it will backfire. I'll be seen simply as a scientist pursuing the good of mankind. You, on the other hand, will be seen as an ambitious doctor willing to sacrifice his own child for his career."

Listening in the shadows behind the door, Rachel felt her legs give way beneath her. Forgetting to eat lunch had further weakened her physical state; and now, as Chan recounted the truth about her first pregnancy, a wave of nausea hit her. She bore up, suppressing the urge to vomit, and hoping to hear further revelation. But her strength was gone, her stamina nonexistent. She was fading fast. A light-headedness settled over her, and it was all she could do to prop herself up against the wall. She slid slowly and quietly to the floor. Then everything went white.

CHAPTER 17

Last Straw

The sick feeling in the pit of Matt's stomach was back. His encounter with Chan had left him debilitated—devoid of hope, devoid of direction. He'd been driving home on autopilot, and now he was approaching the house. He turned slowly into the drive, switched off the ignition and sat paralyzed. No denying it—he needed Rachel. He needed to hold her, to kiss her, to feel the warmth of her

body against his. Most of all, he needed to hear her reassuring words. Words of acceptance, words of never-failing loyalty. But as usual, Rachel's car was gone, and the house was
empty; Rachel practically lived at the I.C.N. Matt sauntered
aimlessly through the house, uncertain of his next move.
Then, as he entered his study, the flashing red light of the
answering machine caught his eye. He pressed the button and
a computer-generated voice announced: "You have one message."

An unfamiliar, high-pitched voice drew him in closer.
"Mrs. Hamilton? This is Elise Prescott. I'm sorry for not con-
tacting you earlier, and I know this is unexpected, but I'm at
U.N.C. soccer camp this week, and I'd very much like to
meet you." There was a long pause, then the voice drew a
deep breath and resumed. "My schedule is crazy, but maybe
you can come to one of my scrimmages. We play at 3:00 and
then again at 7:00. Today I'm playing on the field next to
Carmichael Auditorium. Please try to come."

Gripped by a sense of impending doom, Matt stood
motionless—his life unraveling before his eyes. A thick, mental fog settled around him, making it difficult to see, much
less think. He strained to focus, to assess his circumstances:
*Why was this happening? Why had Elise been thrown into the
equation? Weren't Chan's threats enough? Wasn't the certain disso-
lution of his marriage sufficient punishment? Was it just a coincidence that Elise was calling now; or was it, as Rachel would say, an
act of Providence?* Whatever the cause, it was forcing him to

deal with the truth, pushing him into a corner with no exit, no escape. Denial was no longer an option.

Matt wrestled with his thoughts, but eventually curiosity overpowered his apprehension, and he found himself driving towards Carmichael Auditorium. Before he knew it, he was pulling into the narrow drive between Carmichael and the soccer field. He parked quickly, jumped out of the car, and slipped over to the fence—all the while hoping nobody would notice his presence.

There was no way to prepare for what he saw. Matt gasped out loud at the first sight of her, for it had to be Elise; her appearance was a dead giveaway. Matt's breathing stopped altogether, and seconds ticked off before he finally drew another breath. No doubt about it. Elise was a carbon copy of Rachel. It was uncanny. Inconceivable. He watched in awe as the petite dynamo plowed her way to the goal, her auburn ponytail swinging from side to side.

Did Chan really do this? Was Elise the result of a callous experiment, an outcome of the abortion? It was a disturbing theory, but too obvious to dismiss. He knew he must find Rachel. She belonged here. With this girl. . . .

"Matt, what's up?" Helen Bohannon's greeting broke into his world. "Didn't expect to find you watching a soccer game."

"Hey. Didn't see you come up." Matt struggled to hide his alarm at being discovered. "What are you doing here?"

"I asked you first." Helen shot back.

"Just noticed the game, had a few minutes to spare—"

"That'll be the day. Come clean. What's your business here?" Helen quipped.

Matt was shaking, trying hard to contain the rising sense of shame and guilt. His vocal cords were fixed, immovable—preventing him from uttering a sound. But even if the words would come, Matt had no explanation for Helen, no rationale except the truth. His silence spoke volumes.

Realizing something was terribly amiss, Helen stopped pressing for an answer. Then her journalistic sense came into play, "It's Elise isn't it?"

"What?" Matt tried to play dumb. "What are you talking about?"

"The girl out there—Elise Prescott—you know something, don't you?"

"I have no idea what you're getting at," Matt stammered.

"Matt, something's going on. I've tracked her here, and I know she isn't Prescott's biological daughter. Dr. MacKenzie told me about their blood types not matching. You know, too, don't you?"

Matt stared in astonishment but said nothing.

Helen continued, almost as if she were talking to herself. "She looks so familiar. I know I've seen her before. But where?" Helen's voice trailed off momentarily as she tried to recall a chance meeting with Elise. Then she resumed her questioning. "Matt, you've got to let me in on what you know. I can't help if I don't have all the facts. This has something to do with the past you're trying to hide, doesn't it?"

226

Matt broke eye contact and dropped his head.

"Matt, please tell me . . . let me help. You were involved with Chan. I know that. What did you do? Did you donate sperm for one of Chan's experiments? Is this girl your offspring?"

"NO! NO!" Matt's retort shot out like rapid fire. "I had nothing to do with this . . . I . . . I . . . didn't know. I—" His voiced cracked in midsentence.

Helen glanced over at Elise while Matt composed himself, then her face registered a shocked look. "My God, Matt. Elise looks like a woman I met in MacKenzie's office. Her name was a biblical one . . . I know. I know it. . . ."

Matt maintained his silence.

"Rachel. Rachel. That's it."

Matt jumped back as if jolted by an electrical shock, and Helen instantly picked up on his reaction.

"Please, Matt. You've got to tell me what you know. Elise's life may be in danger."

Matt raised his head, "What do you mean, her life may be in danger?"

"I've been working with an undercover agent on this. He overheard part of a conversation between Chan and one of his colleagues, and best I understand, these guys intend to 'get rid of the evidence.' I thought it was lab evidence of some sort at first. But it's Elise, isn't it? She's the evidence they're talking about?"

"OK." Matt spit out his reply, his exasperation mounting. "You're right. Elise is the evidence. But, don't ask me anything else. Not now." Matt spoke with painstaking precision as if to control an emotional outburst threatening to spill out.

"Just let me ask a few more. That's all. You can simply say yes or no. OK?"

Matt reluctantly nodded affirmatively.

"OK. Is this serious enough to warrant putting Elise in protective custody?"

"Yes."

"And the woman I met in MacKenzie's office, you know her, right?"

"Yes—she's . . . my wife."

"Your wife? Matt, you're in deeper than I imagined. Am I right to assume she's connected with Chan's experiment?"

Matt reluctantly nodded.

Helen shook her head in disbelief. "And she doesn't even know, does she?" Helen didn't expect an answer. She spoke definitively, as if finally piecing a puzzle together.

"Not yet—" Matt blurted out defensively, searching Helen's eyes for understanding, for affirmation. He found neither.

"If what you're telling me is true, and if Chan is intent on removing any trace of evidence, then Elise is not the only one whose life may be in danger. Think about your wife. I mean, I wouldn't put anything past Chan—"

Such a threat to Rachel's well-being alarmed Matt, and any lingering self-pity all but evaporated. He quickly cut off

Helen's speculation and refocused on the possible ramifications of Rachel's innocent connection to Chan. "Surely, Chan wouldn't be so . . . so calculating as to—"

"You of all people know what Chan is capable of. I shouldn't have to convince you."

"OK, OK. But Rachel isn't evidence in the strictest sense." Matt qualified his hesitation to buy into Helen's premise. "Still, protective custody isn't a bad idea. Can you arrange protection for Rachel as well?"

"I'll try."

"Well, move on that. I'll find Rachel and—"

Beep, beep, beep. Matt's pager sounded, interrupting his directives. He read the number on the display and gave Helen a pained look. "The ER."

Switching to his doctor mode, Matt assumed a professional demeanor and strode over to his car where he promptly answered the page on his car phone. "This is Dr. Hamilton. Someone paged me?" After listening attentively, he gave an abbreviated reply: "Be right there."

He hung up the phone and turned to Helen, who had followed him over to his car. "Gotta take care of this." Ruefully, he looked back towards the field. "Please follow up. I—"

"Don't worry. I've got it covered." Helen pulled out a small business card and placed it in the palm of Matt's hand and folded his fingers around it, "Here. This is the agent I'm working with. Call him if there's any way he can help."

"Thanks." Matt pocketed the card, then turned the key in the ignition and slowly backed out of the drive. He was torn between going straight to Rachel and responding to the page. He quelled his anguish by reminding himself that Rachel was safe with Leah and that she would remain safe as long as she stayed in the I.C.N. *As long as she stayed there.*

Despite this reassurance, Matt knew he must get to Rachel as soon as possible. It was imperative, not an option. Every fiber in his body knew that. But now, he had to attend to someone else's emergency. *Emergency. I'll give them emergency.* He sped off towards the hospital, snatching one last glimpse of Elise in the process.

CHAPTER 18

The Plan

An eerie stillness surrounded Rachel when she opened her eyes again. The office was dark except for a shaft of moonlight beaming in through the bank of windows, and she had no idea how long she had been out. There was no sign of Matt or Chan. In fact, it seemed she was the only person left in the entire Biotech complex.

She pulled herself up into a sitting position and braced

herself against the wall as she replayed the news about her first pregnancy. Reality hit hard. Trusting Matt implicitly all these years had been easy. She had never doubted his love. But now, his unwavering devotion was in question. He couldn't have truly loved her and deceived her about the miscarriage at the same time. He just couldn't have. Was everything built on a lie, an illusion? Had she been foolish to trust so naively?

Matt had proved his love early on, making the current situation hard to accept. Rachel thought back to the time Matt surprised her with an engagement ring and then wisked her off to meet his father and announce the news. She was still glowing from Matt's proposal and awash with wedding plans when they reached Baltimore. It never occurred to her that the elder Dr. Hamilton would object to their marriage.

Her first impression of Dr. Hamilton was intimidating at best, and immediately she understood why Matt was so intent on pleasing his father; his towering demeanor effortlessly commanded respect. The elder Hamilton responded swiftly to the news, ignoring Rachel and directing his comments to Matt: "Why didn't you consult with me before you took this action?"

"I didn't think it would matter."

"Of course it matters. It will ruin everything. You have your whole life laid out before you—med school, training. Don't think for a moment that jumping into bed with some—" He stopped short of attaching a disparaging label.

"Dad! What are you saying? You don't even know Rachel."

"I know enough, and if your mother were still alive, she'd be aghast. This girl has no breeding whatsoever. She's a gold digger, nothing more."

Completely unprepared for Dr. Hamilton's wholesale rejection, Rachel automatically started backing away, but Matt took hold of her arm and held her firmly in place. Then he looked resolutely at his father and spoke sharply. "You have no right to speak about Rachel like that."

"I have every right. I'm the one footing the bill for your education, remember? And as long as I continue to support you, I have the right to direct your future."

"That may be true in part, but you have no right to determine who I marry."

"Wrong again. You know quite well how your grandfather and I mapped out your future, so if you decide you don't want to be part of that future any more, then go ahead, throw your life away."

"Please give Rachel a chance. Give us a chance! Don't be rash."

"Rash? You call my response rash? I anticipated something like this, and I will not waiver. You know me better than that."

"Are you asking me to choose between you and Rachel?"

"I prefer to call it choosing to fulfill your destiny as a

physician. Mark my words, you'll never finish your training if you marry now."

"I can do both. I shouldn't be forced to choose."

"Well then, choose both, but don't expect any help from me. You marry this girl, and I promise you, you won't get a cent from me."

"But I love her!"

"And marrying for love is always trouble."

"You can't mean that."

"Just try me."

Despite the past, it was now clear that Matt had openly deceived her. It was an unfathomable act, especially from the one to whom she had given her heart freely and lovingly. "Our whole relationship has been a lie," Rachel wept out loud. *How did I miss seeing the truth? Surely there were signs. How could I have been so blind?* She doubled over, clutched her abdomen and then proceeded to vomit on the clean, white, tile floor. Her heart froze. She felt nothing.

For a long while she sat on the tile, slowly rocking back and forth with her arms wrapped tightly around her knees. It hurt too much to think. And all she really wanted to do was to forget, to block out the whole shocking revelation.

Finally, the dam broke, unleashing anger. But surprisingly, her anger was not alone—a tinge of elation was also working its way to the surface. The miscarriage had yielded a daughter—Elise no less—and that fact in itself was validating. Her sixth sense was accurate; the connection was real.

She wasn't crazy or delusional after all. In fact, she was perfectly sane.

Yet how should she respond? Should she celebrate having another child, or vent her anger at Matt, or both? Uncertainty reigned. Clearly, she didn't understand why Matt gave into Chan so many years ago, and it was impossible to reconstruct his frame of mind. But now he sounded sorry. Now, he was trying to protect her. But was that enough to erase the hurt? Her confusion mounted.

She looked around the darkened room and drank up the sacred solitude, associating the feeling with a time, years before, when she was a little girl—alone in a vast, Gothic sanctuary. It was Wednesday afternoon again. Choir practice was over. She had broken away from the other girls, sneaking into the penetrating stillness of the stone-walled sanctuary, her footsteps echoing off the walls, a mystical force drawing her in further. The sense of belonging was real. The sense of God's presence was staggering, yet responding to the calling seemed natural and right. She raised her eyes, captivated momentarily by a pattern painted on a stained-glass window. Then she bowed her head and prayed—innocently and unrestrained—as any child might have done.

Tonight, at Biotech, God's presence was close again. Praying was inevitable. Rachel dropped to her knees and cried out loud: "Oh Father, I have been gone so long. Please forgive me. I feel so alone, so hurt. Only you can fill the hole in my heart. Please help me. Give me strength, give me wisdom to know how to respond to Matt. Help me find it in my heart to forgive him."

Rachel poured out her tears until she was empty. An eternity seemed to pass, then she stood up and searched her heart once more. Matt had broken her trust. That was a fact. Yet she didn't harbor hate, only sadness. An intense anger burned within but now it was directed at Chan. Was it righteous anger? She couldn't tell. She questioned her motives: Why was it easier to lash out at Chan? Was it because Chan was the monster, not her husband?

The thought of retaliating against Chan gained momentum. Rachel weighed her options, mulling over the circumstances before her. Then a strategy began to take shape. She would join Matt in his fight against Chan. They could beat him at his own game if they worked together. *How providential . . . alone at Biotech. . . .* It would be a simple matter to find evidence against Chan; the evidence needed, as Matt had said, "to nail him."

Nothing in Chan's office stood out as potentially damaging. A cursory review of his files did not yield anything helpful, and Rachel realized that detailed descriptions of his activities would most likely be located in the clinic area. Finding incriminating evidence would require searching through dozens of charts, and that would take time. Time she didn't have. She was about to give up the search when she noticed a videotape cued into a VCR, ready to play. She turned on the TV, pushed the play button and watched in astonishment as Dr. Chan appeared on the screen, lecturing a group of doctors. Rachel increased the volume and listened attentively:

The demand for fetal tissue continues to rise. We have an opportunity—an obligation—with the new technologies available, to allay the ramifications of certain disease processes and prevent others all together. It is an exciting time to be practicing medicine. The frontiers we now cross will impact generations to come.

Today, I plan to share two procedures: First is a procurement procedure, which ensures intact fetal tissue in the late stages of pregnancy. Second is a technique I have perfected by combining aborted fetal tissue with an egg procured from the ovary of the same fetus. These procedures have allowed me to produce an identical twin. Although "cloning" is a more accurate term, I prefer "twin," as it does not carry the same negative connotations.

Let me explain the procedure: First, the nucleus from a cell—any cell from the fetal tissue—is fused with an electric current to the unfertilized egg obtained from the fetal ovary. Properly preparing the fetal ovum for this proce- dure is imperative. In order to accelerate the mat- uration process, the immature egg or ova is injected with various hormones. Once ripe, the nucleus of the egg is removed and replaced with the nucleus of the other cell by the fusion process I mentioned earlier. This egg, now equipped with a nucleus, grows into an embryo which can be implanted into a willing carrier—usually a woman unable to have children of her own. The offspring, or progeny, is a child, which is the identical twin of the aborted fetus.

The benefits of producing an identical twin as I have described are numerous. Organ replace- ment is one. Even though the process of harvest- ing fetal tissue immediately after abortion already provides organs for transplantation, having a "fetal farm," so to speak, will enable mass pro- duction on a wider scale and enable researchers to discover new and broader applications.

Startled by the sound of a nearby door opening and closing, Rachel quickly pushed eject and then the power tab to off. Intently, she seized the videotape out of the VCR, then reached over and clicked off the desk lamp. In her haste, she fumbled, dropping the video on the floor. Not waiting for her eyes to adjust to the darkness, she fell to her knees and frantically began scouring the floor, knowing it was crucial to get that tape into the right hands.

Groping around in the dark only intensified her panic. Finally, she located the teaching tape and shoved it into her shoulder bag just as the glare of a flashlight blinded her, and a deafening voice demanded, "What are you doing in here?"

Rachel's heart leaped within her chest.

CHAPTER 19

Sin
Sick

Abroad set of steel doors flung open as Matt hastened into the ER from the ambulance ramp. Dodging a stretcher in route to the OR, Matt ducked under IV tubing strung between a wheelchair-bound patient and an IV pole which an orderly pushed sluggishly along. Although the orderly lifted the tubing as high as he could reach, Matt was still forced to contort his body to pass beneath it.

When he finally scooted past the obstacle course and strode down the narrow corridor towards the nurse's station, he saw several nurses standing at attention as if awaiting his arrival. As he drew closer, they lowered their heads, returned to their individual tasks, and ignored his presence. Matt leaned over the counter in an attempt to regain their attention. "I'm here. Someone want to fill me in on the psych admit?"

A nurse looked up, her sober expression alerting Matt to the gravity of the situation. She said nothing, just grabbed a chart and motioned for Matt to follow her.

"From what I gathered over the phone, this is the same student we saw about a month ago?"

"Correct." The nurse stopped briefly, turning around to respond. Her face was a familiar one, but Matt was unable to put a name with it. He strained to read the identification badge pinned to her lab coat: Susan Harrison, RN, Unit Manager.

"The counselor from student health brought her over," she continued. "Seems the student developed tachycardia during her weekly session, and the counselor panicked."

"Didn't we have her on Ativan?"

"According to the chart, yes. But whether she was actually taking it, we don't know."

"Why did the counselor—"

"Ask her yourself. She's in here." Susan pulled back a curtain, revealing a harried woman and an emaciated, hollow-eyed young girl thrashing around on the bed.

242

"Hi. I'm Dr. Hamilton." Matt extended his hand to the woman seated beside the bed. "I believe we've talked on the phone."

"Yes. Marcia Collier, from student health." She stood to greet him then sunk back into the chair.

"Looks like you've had a rough time of it here."

"You're right on that one. I'm definitely out of my league—totally unprepared."

"Want to fill me in?"

"I've been seeing Angie," she pointed to the girl, "for anxiety attacks. She said her problem was stress related—exams. But just one look at her, and I knew she was anorexic. Of course, she hasn't admitted to that, but like I said, it was pretty obvious. Anyway, she came in today, and we were starting to deal with some family issues when she started hyperventilating and then just collapsed on the floor, saying she felt like her heart would beat right out of her chest."

"Did she say anything about taking her Ativan?"

"Not a word. But the heart-rate problem is not what concerns me. What I witnessed was the closest thing I've ever seen to D.I.D.—she kept flipping back and forth between different personalities. I tried to ask questions, but she would just scream, 'I'm not allowed to talk with you.' I was getting nowhere, so here we are."

Matt looked pensive, then walked over to the bedside and spoke directly to the girl. "Angie, I'm Dr. Hamilton. Can you talk with me a minute?"

The girl stopped thrashing momentarily and then stared blankly into Matt's eyes. "I can't. I'm not allowed."

"What do you mean, you're not allowed?" Matt lowered his voice and crouched down next to her.

"She won't let me."

"Who won't let you?"

Angie started to speak but then froze. She looked terrified. "I can't tell."

Matt gently took her hand. "You don't have to be afraid. I'm not going to let anything happen to you."

"You don't understand. She'll hurt me." Angie pointed to some deep scratches on her forearm.

"Who did this to you?"

"I can't tell you," she meekly responded.

"Listen, I can't help you if you don't tell me who it is." Matt's approach was firm but kind. "You have to tell me."

The girl searched Matt's face and then in a barely detectable whisper stammered, "The dark . . . the dark one. She gives out the punishment to me and the other children."

"What other children?"

"The children inside my head."

Matt glanced over at the counselor, who simply raised her hands, palms up, in dismay. Then he turned back to Angie and spoke tenderly. "We're going to let you stay here for the night. We want you to be safe. Someone will be nearby to help you at all times. OK?"

Without warning, Angie's mouth twisted into a sneer,

and a glare replaced the vacuous look in her eyes. Suddenly a guttural voice scoffed, "You can't help. You can't protect the children. You're a murderer. A murderer!" A demonic laugh followed the accusation.

Matt reeled backwards and all but lost his balance. Susan reached out and grabbed his arm to steady him. "Are you all right?"

"I think so," Matt nodded, then looked over at the counselor. "You did the right thing bringing her in. This is serious." Matt turned back to Susan. "Can you take care of getting her admitted?"

Susan nodded affirmatively.

"Good. I'll go write up the orders."

Dismissing himself, Matt made a beeline into the doctors' lounge. Still shaken by Angie's outburst, he tried to convince himself that her accusation had nothing to do with him personally. He was pouring himself a cup of coffee when Macon showed up.

"Thought I'd find you here."

"How so?"

"I was still in the office finishing up charts when Marcia called to ask what she should do. I told her to bring Angie right in, that you were on call for the ER."

"Thanks for the warning." Matt stared off into space as he remembered his encounter with Helen on the soccer field. *How easy to get caught up in the lives of patients. If I could just keep busy, maybe I wouldn't have to think about Elise.*

"Earth to Matt. Are you in there?"

"Sure."

"Are you OK? You look—"

"I'm fine." Matt quickly offered his typical abbreviated response.

"You could've fooled me." Not realizing the severity of the moment, Macon jokingly added, "Come on, open up. You can trust me, I'm a doctor."

"Andy, it's bad. Really bad."

Macon's expression changed radically. "So tell me."

"The guilt thing." Matt blurted out. "I can't shake it. It's right in my face."

"Same thing we talked about before?"

Matt nodded.

"Wanna be specific this time?"

Matt took a deep breath and proceeded to unload, "Years ago I deceived Rachel . . . and . . . and . . . as you know, 'out of sight, out of mind' worked fine for me. I've never really been *forced* to deal with it. Sure, it's surfaced from time to time, but I was able to put it aside. But things are different now."

"How so?"

"Now I have Prescott's daughter showing up to haunt me, to remind me of the past. Then to top it off, a psychotic patient spews accusations at me, calls me a murderer! I realize she doesn't know what she's saying, but—things are totally out of control."

246

"Slow down, Matt. You'll have to fill in the blanks if you want me to understand."

"I've done something totally unacceptable, totally unforgivable."

"Unforgivable?"

"Yes. There's no way anyone could forgive this."

Macon maintained eye contact and solemnly nodded for Matt to continue.

"You know I used to work for Chan?" Matt paused, waiting for Macon's response.

Again Macon simply nodded for Matt to proceed.

"Well, I helped set up an . . . an—" Matt couldn't bring himself to say the word *abortion*. At first he looked down, then he raised his head and looked helplessly at Macon, but Macon didn't offer to finish the sentence. Finally, Matt spit out the rest of his confession. "Chan caused her to abort, and Rachel never knew the truth. I lied, I—"

"Are you saying what I think you're saying?"

"Would I make up something like that?"

"No."

"I never thought I could hurt Rachel like this. I never thought I was capable—" Matt lowered his head in shame. His confession was irrevocable.

"Does Rachel have any idea of what really happened?"

Matt looked shocked. "Of course not. I can't tell her. . . . I failed her; I've failed myself."

Macon responded with sober compassion, "You're right.

You did fail her. The guilt you're feeling is valid."

"Don't you think I know that? I'm sick about it. But there's nothing I can do." He dropped down in a chair, bent over, and held his head in his hands.

Macon pulled up a chair next to Matt and faced him. "Matt, I wish I could do something. But I can't. I can't absolve you of your guilt. The only one—"

"I know, I know. I know what you're gonna say. 'The only one that can do that is Christ.'"

"So turn to him. That's all it takes."

"That's easy for you to say. You haven't done what I've done. God could never forgive me. And Rachel won't either. It's over. Rachel's gonna find out. There's no stopping it. She'll never forgive me. Never."

"Matt, I'm no theologian, but I do know that God can and does forgive the most heinous crimes. Every sin is the same in his eyes. We're all on equal footing when it comes to sinning."

"I hear what you're saying. But it doesn't apply to me. God is just too far away. He may be out there somewhere, but I can't reach that far. Besides, even if he could forgive me, Rachel won't. She'll leave me. And I don't blame her at all."

"Like I said, Matt, I can't help you on this. God's the one in the forgiveness business. I wish I *could* get Rachel to forgive you, but I can't. That's God's doing, too. He's the one who enables us to forgive others. Nothing's impossible with him."

"But it can't be that easy. God can't let me off the hook for what I did, can he?"

"He doesn't let you off the hook; he's arranged for someone else to pay the price. That's where Christ comes in."

Matt looked earnestly at Macon. "You seem so sure of that. So confident. Why is it so easy for you to believe that?"

"I suppose it's a faith thing. You trust God to tell the truth, to keep his promise."

"But when you're not sure there's even a God out there, how can you trust him?"

"Oh, you know he's out there all right. Everyone knows he's out there. They just suppress that knowledge or else they create their own god—a god they can control. If you ask me, it's just easier to acknowledge him in the first place."

"I don't know, I don't know anything." Matt shook his head and mumbled more to himself than to Macon. "It would be a miracle if Rachel forgave me."

"Like I said Matt, I can't help you on that one."

"Well, if what you're saying is true, if God can get Rachel to forgive me, then just maybe there's something to what you're saying."

"Better be careful. Don't go setting up conditions for God to meet."

"I'm just saying I'd see it as God reaching down to me."

"But He's already done that. Don't you see?"

"I don't see a lot right now, Macon. It's all hazy. Give me some time." Matt stood up, straightened his lab coat, and assumed the role of doctor again. "Right now I've gotta get going. Talk with you later?"

"Later." Macon watched as Matt turned and exited the lounge. Then he looked up and sighed. "It's in your hands."

───────────

After making sure that Angie was settled in the psych unit, Matt refocused his attention on the matter of Rachel's safety. He headed towards the I.C.N., not knowing how he would broach the subject of the past and Elise. Sharon greeted him as he entered the scrub area. "Hi, Dr. Hamilton. Coming to see your daughter?" The young nurse flashed a familiar smile.

"Ah . . . yes."

"Well, have a nice visit. And by the way, tell your wife we missed her at Tommy's one-month birthday party."

"That's not all she missed," Dr. MacKenzie announced as she strode into the doorway. "She stood me up for coffee."

"What are you guys talking about?" Matt queried, searching both their faces for a hint of an explanation.

MacKenzie spoke first. "I saw her several hours ago, on her way over to your office. She was supposed to meet me in the coffee shop afterwards but never showed."

"Well, she never came back here either, and she missed a great party," Sharon said.

"She's not here?" Matt was completely taken aback.

"That's the point," MacKenzie confirmed.

"What was she going to my office for?"

"She said something about needing to talk with you about an ethical issue," Sharon concluded, then made her way out the doorway. "I really have to get going. Hope you find her."

"Guess I'll retrace her steps," Matt sighed, making an about-face. *Where in the world could she be this time of night?*

"Tell her she owes me." MacKenzie called out after him.

CHAPTER 20

Confrontation

"My dear Rachel, so glad you could drop by." Chan's saccharine voice reverberated as he entered the office behind the security guard. "Thanks for letting me know about our little intruder, Hank. Restrain her, and I'll notify the police." The guard momentarily loosened his constricting grip on Rachel's arm and pulled out a pair of handcuffs. He jerked her around, forced her into a chair, and then cuffed her to it. Chan motioned for the guard to leave. "I'll handle things from here." The guard nodded and left.

Chan turned his attention to Rachel. "So, thought you'd put your investigative skills to work . . . do a bit of digging?"

"I'll dig up whatever I can to nail you. What you're doing is illegal."

"On the contrary, my dear. The research I'm doing is quite legal. You're the one breaking the law. Breaking and entering, trespassing on private property."

"I didn't break and enter; the doors were open. I simply fainted, that's all."

"How do you explain your presence in my office? Looks like trespassing to me, and I'm sure it will look like that to the authorities as well. So what did your little investigation reveal?"

Rachel knew Chan was baiting her, and she wasn't about to give him any indication that her search was successful. She gave Chan a helpless, innocent look while offering an explanation: "I was looking for a clock. I had no idea what time it was. It was late, and I knew Matt would be worried. I was about to call him when your security guard began manhandling me. So rude."

Chan glared at her and ordered, "Dispense with the charade. What were you doing in this building?"

"I followed my husband . . . heard you pressuring him. Heard how you lied to me."

"I presume you also heard how Matt was a willing participant in arranging—"

"Yes, I heard."

"And the betrayed wife has no objections?" Chan twisted the knife deeper, hoping to alienate her from Matt.

"This is something we'll have to work out. It's none of your business."

"Oh, but it is my business. You and Matt have become, shall we say, irritants? My partners aren't nearly as gracious as I, and they demand a rapid resolution. They view your continued meddling in our affairs as a fly that needs swatting. I warned Matt. Offered him a way to redeem himself in the eyes of my associates, but as you evidently know, he refused. Foolish decision."

"He'll never give in to you. Never."

"He made that very clear. That's why we've decided to go forward with our plan."

"Plan?"

"Oh, yes. You will be silenced. And Matt, if he refuses to cooperate, will see an end to his career." Chan pulled a syringe out of his lab coat pocket and moved closer to Rachel.

"What do you think you're doing?" Rachel cried.

"Just as I said. I'm silencing you. Putting an end to your interference. And Matt should be sufficiently subdued after it's discovered that his wife overdosed on the very drugs he prescribed for her. What a tragedy. I'm sure this will convince him to cooperate."

Chan withdrew medication from a small vial and tapped the syringe in preparation for the injection. Rachel struggled against the handcuffs but found it useless; her weakness was no match for the metal restraints. He held her arm steady and injected the drug into her upper arm. "Just relax, my dear. I've got things completely under control," Chan laughed cruelly. "You made this so easy for us. The moment the security guard called and told me you were here, I knew the timing was perfect." He reached across his desk, picked up the phone and dialed 911. "Yes, this is Dr. Robert Chan at Biotech in Research Triangle. We found a former patient wandering the halls, apparently drugged and incoherent. Could you please send an ambulance? That's right . . . top floor."

Chan folded his arms and paced around the office as if contemplating his next move. He stopped briefly by Rachel's bag and she cringed, praying, *Please God, don't let him find the tape.* Finally deciding Rachel was no longer a threat, Chan removed the handcuffs and dropped them into his top desk drawer.

Rachel knew it was only a matter of minutes before the drug took effect. She deliberately slowed her breathing, counting each breath as if it were her last. . . .

Just a few scattered vehicles dotted the horizon as Matt turned his Scout into a near-empty Biotech parking lot. The closer he drove to the buildings, the more distinguishable the lone Volvo wagon became. Rachel's car! He pulled up alongside and surveyed the Volvo's interior. Even in the dim moonlight, Matt recognized her books and papers strung out across the backseat. *I was right. She saw my appointment book and followed me here.*

He parked and then sprinted to the front entrance, stopping dead in his tracks when he found the doors locked. *Don't know why I thought they'd be open this time of night.* He rattled the glass doors in hopes of alerting someone to his presence. *Surely, there's a security guard around here somewhere.* But not a soul appeared. He ran from door to door, calling out for help and rattling every door along the front of the building. *Somebody has to hear all this commotion.* Again, no response.

Determined not to panic, Matt returned to his car, grabbed his car phone, then reached into his pocket and retrieved the card Helen had given him. Quickly dialing the number on the card, he steadied himself as a husky voice answered.

"Detective Henson here."

"This is Dr. Matt Hamilton. Helen Bohannon gave me your number."

"Yes, Dr. Hamilton, Helen said you might be calling."

"I need your help."

"Sure. How can I help?"

"I think Chan has my wife. I mean, I'm sure he has my wife. I'm out at Biotech, and I can't get in and—"

"Hold on. Where did you say you were?"

"Research Triangle Park—Biotech complex."

"OK. Now what's this about your wife?"

"She's not at the hospital, her car is here. Chan has her. I know—"

"Settle down. We don't know anything at this point. You can't prove she's in there with Chan, can you?"

"Well, no, but—"

"But nothing. For all we know, she parked there and went off with someone."

"It could be Chan."

"Listen, Dr. Hamilton, I'm all for helping, and there's nothing I'd like better than to catch Chan in some criminal activity, but exactly how can I help in this situation?"

"You can get me into this facility. You can help me find Rachel."

"Just hold your horses. We'll need a search warrant to enter the premises, and no judge is gonna grant one when you don't have anything more specific to go on."

"I don't have time to beg. Either you help me, or you don't. I've wasted enough time already. I'm breaking in."

"Listen up, Doc. At least wait until I can get over there. If you set off an alarm, the cops will be all over you in a matter of minutes."

"If that's what it takes to get someone's attention, so be it." Matt slammed the receiver down and then went around to the back of his vehicle and lifted a jack out of the floorboard compartment. He raced back over to the front entrance, his tire jack in tow, and with one hefty swing, heaved the car jack into the door. The collision shattered glass everywhere, and almost immediately, an alarm went off, blasting the stillness of the previously silent night.

Matt carefully stepped through the broken glass and made his way over to the elevator, impatiently pushing the up button several times. *What's taking so long? It should have been here by now.* Suddenly, a loud voice bellowed across the lobby, "Hold it right there buddy. What do you think you're doing in here?"

Matt looked around to see a heavyset, gray-haired security guard approaching him. He glanced back at the unresponsive elevator and then made an instant decision. He ducked into the nearby stairwell and bounded up the first two flights of stairs. Hearing the guard following close behind, he reached the third floor landing and pulled open the fire door. He ran down the hallway, looking frantically for another stairwell. Rounding a corner, he saw the exit sign marking another stairwell. Without slowing, Matt raced toward it. He flung open the door and quickly shot up the next several flights without a trace of the security guard following behind.

Once he reached the top floor, Matt made his way down the familiar corridor toward Chan's office—the only one with the lights on. Without hesitation, he rushed through the open doorway and discovered Rachel seated in a chair in plain sight. Relieved to find her unharmed, he hurried to her side. Ignoring Chan's presence, he knelt down—his face inches from hers—and whispered, "What are you doing here?"

"I followed you."

"I know. I ran into MacKenzie and then went to my office and figured it out. But why are you still here?"

"Fainted after hearing you and Chan."

"You heard?"

"Everything."

"Oh Babe, I'm sorry . . . so sorry!" He dropped his head, and his voice broke. He tried to continue speaking, but Rachel put her finger to his lips, "Ssshh. Not now." Her words began to slur. "Drugs . . . Chan—" Then with an urgency and her last ounce of strength, she clutched his arm and mouthed, "My bag." Then her eyes closed, and her body went limp, slumping down in the chair.

Matt jumped up and grabbed Chan by the collar, "What have you done?"

Chan calmly, but firmly, loosened Matt's grip from his shirt. He spoke as if in total control. "Matt, why do you act so surprised? You had your chance. It's over. You're too late."

"What do you mean, 'I'm too late'?"

"You refused to work with us. You forced us to contain the situation. We had no other choice." Chan glanced over at Rachel and continued. "Your dear wife has just overdosed on the very drugs you've been treating her with for over a decade. It's not going to look good for you. I'm sure there will be an investigation into how you illegally wrote prescriptions for controlled substances."

Dazed in disbelief, Matt tried to absorb what Chan was saying. Before he could respond, two police officers barged into the office with their weapons drawn.

"Don't move!" They gave the room a quick once-over and then demanded, "What's going on in here?"

Chan turned innocently towards them, his shoulders shrugged and palms up in the air. "Officers, I've just called 911. This woman has a history of drug abuse and paranoid behavior. Tonight she made an unauthorized entry and, as you can see, is anything but stable. You might find it helpful to question her husband here about her drug problem."

As Chan spoke, Matt returned to Rachel's side and monitored her barely detectable breathing. The police turned to Matt and asked questioningly, "Is this true? Does your wife have a drug problem?"

"No! I mean . . . not really. She's taken barbiturates in the past, but this is different. . . . Chan is responsible for this."

Chan interjected, "Officers, Mrs. Hamilton was not invited here. In fact, I have no idea what she's doing here. If you will check, you'll find she's done this sort of thing before. Dr. Hamilton is well aware of previous incidents and has been urged—on several occasions—to control his wife's deranged behavior."

Again, the officers looked to Matt for an explanation,

but Matt was preoccupied. He was administering mouth to mouth resuscitation to Rachel, who had stopped breathing altogether. In the background an ambulance siren wailed. Matt knew his story probably wouldn't convince the officers, but even if they would've believed him, he couldn't stop to explain, not now. *It isn't what it appears. There's more to this.*

The officers turned back to Chan. "Doctor, we'll need to get a statement from you. Do you intend to press charges?"

"No, not now. I don't think Mrs. Hamilton will be bothering anyone for quite a while. It's such a shame." He shook his head, feigning pity, then walked over to the doorway and directed the arriving ambulance attendants to Rachel.

"I'll take over from here," one of the attendants said as he gently pulled Matt away from Rachel.

Matt's pent-up rage spewed forth as he directed his energies toward Chan. "You disgusting animal. You won't get away with this!" His rage grew in intensity. "If it's the last thing I do, you won't get away with this. I promise you that!" Then, casting off all restraint, Matt lunged towards Chan.

The policemen pried Matt away from Chan and held him back as they all stood by helplessly and watched the paramedics intubate Rachel and force oxygen into her lungs. Remembering her request, Matt casually picked up Rachel's bag and placed it beside her, then instructed the paramedics, "Treat this as a drug overdose. Probably IM injection of pentobarbital." As they wheeled Rachel out on a stretcher, Matt leaned over, kissed her tenderly and offered reassurance, "We'll beat this. Just like everything else. You can't leave us. We're a family now. . . ."

―――――――――

It was an all-night vigil for Matt as he anguished in the emergency room. When they first brought Rachel in, most of his time was spent pacing the floor. Now he sat alone, dejected and detached from the chaos. Unable to rest, he couldn't escape his thoughts. The memory of Chan's feigned concern infuriated him. Macon was right, Chan was an evil man. Any illusions about Chan's concern for humanity had long sense been replaced by disdain, and now the calculated attempt to silence Rachel had heightened his contempt for the man. Although he knew it wouldn't be easy, Matt determined to shine a light on Chan's dark side. *But no one will believe the story about Chan injecting Rachel with pentobarbital, much less the story about his dealings with the Chinese. . . .* Exposing Chan would mean fighting a colossal battle.

Thoughts of Elise played over and over in his mind as well. She was not the Prescott's daughter. No debate there. He remembered all too well what Chan had bragged about in his office earlier that day: *I did a little experiment with the fetal ovaries I salvaged from the abortion. . . .* Chan had no right to their fetus, no right to exploit their crisis for his own purposes. It was unconscionable. *I've got to get her back, she belongs*

*with us—her mother, father, and sister. Whatever it takes, I've got to
do it; I've got to restore Elise into our family. I owe Rachel that
much.*

"Matt! Are you all right?" Matt looked up into compassionate green eyes and slowly reoriented himself. It was
Helen. The wall clock behind her read 4:00 A.M..

"I guess so."

"I came as soon as I heard. Is Rachel going to make it?"

"We don't know. They've done all they can at this point.
They're waiting for her blood pressure to stabilize. *I'm* waiting for her to regain consciousness."

"What are they saying about that?"

"No guarantees."

"Oh Matt, I'm so sorry. They said she took an overdose,
but I didn't buy that. What really happened?"

"It was Chan. He did it, but he's covered his tracks so
well no one will believe otherwise. He's made sure of that."

"Listen Matt. Now's not the time to give up. We're so
close."

"I'm not giving up, but you tell me, how do we beat this
guy? He's got all the cards."

"No, he doesn't. He can't. All we have to do is keep the
heat on. Public scrutiny will destroy him. That's been my plan
all along—expose, expose, expose. And now I have the evidence I've been looking for. Now I have Elise."

"No!"

"No? What do you mean by that?"

"We can't drag Elise into this and make her into some kind of freak. I refuse to let that happen."

"Well, we really don't have a choice. Unless you have some other way to expose—"

"Wait! There's a videotape—a Biotech tape. They found it in Rachel's purse when they were searching for drugs. Maybe that's—"

"—what we're looking for!" Helen finished his sentence, then continued with a barrage of her own questions: "Do you still have it? How can I get it?"

———————

Knowing he deserved Rachel's anger, retribution, even rejection, Matt braced himself for the worst as he made his way up to her hospital room the following day. Although relieved to learn her physical condition was under control, Matt feared her psychological state was not nearly as stable. Rachel now knew the truth about the abortion, and Matt dreaded the consequences.

Hoping to avoid the inevitable confrontation as long as possible, Matt vowed not to bring up the past and forced a smile as he stepped through the doorway into her room. When Rachel heard him enter, she immediately turned to face him. The minute her eyes met his, Matt felt his heart skip a beat. He did so love her—loved her ability to see past his ego, loved the sense of permanency she provided. It was an abiding love, the kind you knew would always be with you. Yet Matt knew things would be different now. And although he desperately wanted to make up for the years his schooling had stolen, the years he had withdrawn, he knew it was too late.

He reached her bedside, hid his despair, and leaned over to kiss her gently on the mouth. Then he sat down on the bed beside her.

"You know," he began lightheartedly, "you're spending way too much time at the hospital these days."

"Kind of like role reversal," Rachel quipped in response. "But now *I'm* the one 'living' at the hospital." She flashed a knowing look, then continued her commentary. "There's one minor difference though, I'm not a slave to the system."

"You're a slave to no one!"

"This is a true thing."

There was an awkward silence, then Matt spoke, changing the tone of the conversation. "Last night really scared me. I thought I might lose you."

"And that worried you?" Rachel prodded.

"You know it did." Matt maintained his serious tone. "I can't bear the thought of going through life without you. And—" He tried to stop himself, but couldn't. "And—I know you probably don't feel the same way anymore . . . not after what I did." He looked away from her searching eyes, then forced himself to finish. "And I don't blame you. I don't blame you if you never want to see me again. What I did is unforgivable."

"Darling," Rachel smiled warmly and took his hand in hers. "Remember when you asked me if there was anything I couldn't forgive you for?"

"Yes."

"And what did I say?"

"You said, 'Nothing.'"

"OK then, that still goes. I meant what I said."

"But how . . . why . . . I don't deserve it—"

"None of us do."

Epilogue

The chair rocked rhythmically, keeping beat with the melody softly playing in the background. Holding a small child in her arms, Rachel repositioned the baby on her lap, locked eyes, and then sustained an intense gaze. The child responded excitedly with a heart-melting grin, flailing her arms and legs.

"Leah, Leah, Leah. Your mother loves you so much!"

P r o g e n y

Rachel leaned forward and kissed her daughter on the fore-head. "Today is a special day. Your sister is coming to visit. Your father is picking her up at the airport this very minute." Leah gurgled and smiled, then squirmed to get down on the floor. Rachel leaned over and carefully placed her on a blan-ket, allowing Leah the freedom to practice her latest feat—rolling over.

Rachel seized the opportunity to glance into the mirror, check her lipstick, and quickly run a hairbrush through her shoulder-length hair. *Matt always did like it long.* Her eyes stopped momentarily at the fresh daisies—a gift from Matt—arranged in a crystal vase and prominently displayed on the dresser. Then she heard the clock on the fireplace mantle sound its chimes. Time for the 6:00 news.

Leah screeched in delight as she reached for her toes. "Sssh. . . ." Rachel said as she clicked on the television, strain-ing to hear the newscaster above Leah's squeals and the music still drifting in from the other room.

> Today the senate subcommittee investigating ethics violations questioned Dr. Robert Chan of Biotechnologies Research International. Specific allegations stem from his cloning experiments and fetal tissue procurement. As Biotech receives millions of dollars in research grants from the National Institutes of Health, Dr. Chan's testi-mony is critical in determining whether those moneys will be withdrawn.

Thus far, the investigation has been a hotly contested issue between antiabortion activists and scientists who maintain that instituting restrictions on research will halt strides in curing Parkinson's disease, Alzheimer's disease, juvenile diabetes, spinal cord and other brain injuries. Organ transplant recipients, coming alongside researchers, have demanded that funding for research continue as it stands to benefit at least five million patients. Proabortion advocates, focusing on the benefits of current research efforts, claim that fetal brain and pancreatic cells, which would otherwise be discarded, have been used to extend the lives of thousands of people and improve the quality of life for many more.

Antiabortion activists, calling for moral renewal, are currently staging a prayer vigil on behalf of the fetuses used for research. Thousands of pro-lifers are gathered, protesting what they term a holocaust. Family Protection Council chairman, Warren Still, has expressed outrage, comparing researchers with Nazi doctors and warning about the cost to society if current practices continue. Correspondent Mike Mercer will pick up that story on the steps of the Capitol.

But first, in a related story, Dr. and Mrs. Matthew Hamilton of Chapel Hill, North

Carolina, filed suit today against Biotech for the unlawful use of fetal tissue. An unprecedented custody battle is expected. Also named in the lawsuit are Dr. Forrest Prescott, director of operations for Biotech, and Dr. Robert Chan. The attorney general's office is also investigating possible criminal activity."

Acknowledgments

Progeny's existence is due in large part to the tremendous support I received from some very special friends. Initial prodding to tackle this project came from Pam Render and Kate Huntington. Their excitement fueled my efforts and gave me the confidence to continue. Pam freely offered her insight into the world of fiction and was there for me daily.

Crucial critiques of early drafts came from Skip Cornbrooks and Kristie Kiessling. As I approached the finish line, Karen Brown coached me, challenging me to produce my best work. Then there were Ralph and Lorna Bennie, who consistently prayed for my efforts; John Render, who provided legal details; and Scott Wilcox, police protocol. Of course, my intimate exposure to the medical world came from my heart surgeon–husband of twenty-six years. Most important, I am indebted to my Creator God, who gave me the passion to write and whose grace continues to amaze me.

Related

Resources

The Center for BIOETHICS and Human Dignity
2065 Half Day Road
Brannockburn, IL 60015
800-417-9999
www.bioethix.org

Project Rachel
National Office of Post Abortion Reconciliation and Healing
St. John's Center
3680 Kinnickinnic Avenue
Milwaukee, WI 53207
800-5WE-CARE
www.marquette.edu/rachel/

P.A.C.E.—Post Abortion Counseling & Education
c/o CARENET
101 West Broad Street
Falls Church, VA 22046
800-395-HELP

HEALING HEARTS
P.O. Box 7890
Bonnie Lake, WA 98390
888-217-8679
www.web-light.com/heart/

P r o g e n y

Institute for Pregnancy Loss
111 Bow Street
Portsmouth, NH 03801-3819
603-431-1904

Women at Risk
P.O. Box 7375
Springfield, IL 62791-7375
217-525-5879
www.afterabortion.org

WEBA—Women Exploited by
Abortion
P.O. Box 278
Dawson, TX 76639
817-578-1681

Ramah International, Inc.
1050 Galley Square
Colorado Springs, CO 80915
719-537-7707
Sydna@aol.com

MARC Ministries
(Men's Abortion Recovery)
c/o Wayne Brauning
237 South 13th Avenue
Coatsville, PA 19320
610-384-3210

Fathers and Brothers
350 Broadway, Suite 40
Boulder, CO 80303
303-494-3282

Men Receiving Post Abortion
Counseling
www.hope-net.com/survey_men.html

Men's Post Abortion Help
800-766-2727